Her own Mr. Darcy was pretty much looking like manna from heaven right now.

Gabrielle was lucky. She'd never had the same pressure her brother had—to find the perfect partner, settle down, marry and get ready to run a country.

Sixteen years of spotlight being the perfect princess in Mirinez had been enough. Medicine had been considered an "honorable" profession and she'd climbed on that plane to study medicine at Cambridge University breathing a huge sigh of relief. Since then she'd only returned for weddings, funerals and a few state events. Mirinez had lost interest in her. She hadn't been in press reports for years. And that was exactly the way she wanted it to stay.

She pulled out a chair at the table and gestured for Sullivan to sit down. "Let's focus on what needs to get done in the next two weeks."

She shot him a smile. He stepped closer. His chest was barely inches from her nose and she caught a whiff of pure pheromones. Oh, she could pretty it up by saying it was a combination of soap, remnants of musk antiperspirant and some subtle cologne. But from the effect it was having on her senses it was 100 percent testosterone.

He didn't seem worried about their closeness. In fact, she could almost bet that he thrived on it. The thin material covering his broad chest brushed against her arm as he sat down. "Like I said, tell me what you need, and I'm your guy."

Dear Reader,

I really enjoyed writing *The Doctor and the Princess*—partly due to the fact I got to make up two countries, and partly because I got to write my first princess doctor!

Gabrielle isn't supposed to take over her principality (and you do know that all made-up principalities are secretly Monaco!) but her brother has abdicated and she has no other choice. She hasn't exactly shared the fact she's a princess with her doctor colleagues, and the arrival of her security staff at the exact moment she's about to get up close and personal with her own Mr. Darcy causes a stir.

Sullivan Darcy is the perfect hero, right down to his flaws. He's a doctor who has served in the army and now works for Doctors Without Borders. The attraction between him and Gabrielle is pretty much instant. But beneath the surface Sullivan isn't as smooth as he seems. He lost his dad two years ago and hasn't taken time to grieve. His brain keeps pushing things away—he's a doctor, he's a guy, he shouldn't be feeling like this. In this day and age depression is better recognized and known. It can affect anyone, of any sex, at any age and at any point in their life. That's what I wanted to reflect in this story.

It turns out that Sullivan Darcy needs Gabrielle just as much as she needs him.

I love to hear from readers. Please feel free to contact me via my website, scarlet-wilson.com.

Love,

Scarlet Wilson

THE DOCTOR AND THE PRINCESS

SCARLET WILSON

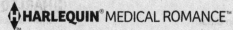

HARLEQUIN® MEDICAL ROMANCE™

Recycling programs
for this product may
not exist in your area.

ISBN-13: 978-0-373-21528-7

The Doctor and the Princess

First North American Publication 2017

Copyright © 2017 by Scarlet Wilson

Printed in U.S.A.

Books by Scarlet Wilson

Harlequin Medical Romance

Christmas Miracles in Maternity
A Royal Baby for Christmas

Midwives On-Call at Christmas
A Touch of Christmas Magic

The Doctor She Left Behind
The Doctor's Baby Secret
One Kiss in Tokyo…

Harlequin Romance

Maids Under the Mistletoe
Christmas in the Boss's Castle

Visit the Author Profile page
at Harlequin.com for more titles.

This book is dedicated to my Australian partners
in crime—Rachael Johns and Emily Madden.
Conferences have never been so much fun!
Can't wait for the next one x

**Praise for
Scarlet Wilson**

"The book is filled with high-strung emotions,
engaging dialogue, breathtaking descriptions and
characters you just cannot help but love. With
the magic of Christmas as a bonus, you won't be
disappointed with this story!"

—*Goodreads* on
A Touch of Christmas Magic

CHAPTER ONE

'IT'S AN EMERGENCY, Sullivan, I swear.'

Sullivan let out a wry laugh as he shook his head and ran his fingers through his damp hair. 'It's *always* an emergency, Gibbs.' He stared at the inside of the khaki tent.

Gibbs laughed too. 'Well, this time it really is. Asfar Modarres collapsed. Some kind of intestinal problem. He was lucky we got him out in time.'

Sullivan started pacing. 'Is he okay?' He liked the Iranian doctor. He'd joined Doctors Without Borders around the same time as Sullivan. They'd never served together but he'd known him well enough to see his commitment and compassion for the job.

'He should be fine. He had surgery a few hours ago.' Gibbs sucked in a deep breath. Sullivan smiled. *Here it comes.*

'Anyway, there's two weeks left of the mission with only one doctor on site. We're at a crucial stage. MDR TB is up to worrying levels in Nambura. We need another pair of hands.'

Sullivan shook his head as he paced. 'I'm a surgeon, Gibbs. Not a medic. Last time I learned about TB I was in med school. I know virtually nothing about it, let alone the multi-drug-resistant strains.'

He wasn't kidding. Ask him to wield a scalpel and he wouldn't hesitate. As an army surgeon he'd operated on the most harrowing injuries, in the most dire of circumstances. No one had ever questioned his surgical abilities. He prided himself on it. But put him in a situation where he wasn't the expert?

'You're a *doctor*, Sullivan—and that's what I need. Anyway, there's no one else I can send.' Gibbs hesitated. 'And there's another issue.'

'What?'

'Nambura can be…difficult.'

Sullivan frowned. 'Spit it out, Gibbs.'

'The medic is Gabrielle Cartier. The two nurses Lucy Provan and Estelle Duschanel, the onsite pharmacist Gretchen Koch.'

Sullivan sucked in a breath and groaned. Four females on their own. Nambura tribes were very traditional. Some of the tribal leaders probably wouldn't even talk to four Western women.

A female colleague had reported minor hostilities on a mission a few months ago. There was no way he'd leave the four of them there for the next two weeks with no back-up. His father would never have left fellow team members at risk and the same principles had been ingrained into Sullivan all his life.

'Okay, you got me. When can you arrange transport?'

Gibbs started talking quickly. 'I'll send you our latest information and protocols on MDR TB. You can read them en route. The helicopter will pick you up in fifty minutes.'

The line went dead as Sullivan stared at the phone. Fifty minutes. Gibbs had clearly already sent the transport before he'd made the call. It was almost as if he'd known Sullivan didn't have anything to go home to.

His top-gun pilot father had died while Sullivan had been on his final tour of duty in Helmand Province. He'd flown home, watched his father buried with full military honours, completed his tour, then had signed up with Doctors Without Borders.

Three years later he'd only managed to go home for nineteen sporadic days. He still hadn't emptied his father's closets or packed up any of his things.

He flung the phone onto his bunk as he pulled his bag from the top of the locker.

Just as well he travelled light.

* * *

The music met his ears as the chopper lifted back up into the black night sky, flattening the trees all around him.

He tilted his head as he tried to recognise the tune and the direction from which it was coming. There was only one path from the landing spot leading through the trees.

He wound his way along it, the music getting louder with every step, until eventually he emerged into a clearing filled with familiar khaki tents identical to the ones he'd left a few hundred miles away and three hours ago.

He glanced around. The set-up rarely varied no matter where they were in the world. A mess tent. Bathrooms and showers. An operation centre and the staff quarters.

A flap was pinned back on the tent that seemed to be the epicentre of the noise. Sullivan's curiosity was piqued.

She had her back to him. Which was just as well as his eyes were immediately drawn to her tanned bare legs. She was wearing a rose pink T-shirt tied in a knot at her hip, revealing the curves of her waist. Her dark hair was in a ponytail that bounced along with her movements. But it was the khaki shorts that had caught his eye. Judging from the frayed edging, they'd obviously once been a pair of trousers and he'd like to shake the hand of the person who had cut them.

On her feet was a pair of heavy black army boots and a pair of rumpled socks. And those legs just kept going and going.

She was bouncing on her toes now. She wasn't just dancing to the beat of Justin Timberlake. Oh, no. She was singing at the top of her voice. And this wasn't just a casual bop about the place. This was a whole dance routine.

He dropped his bag and folded his arms in amusement as she slid from one side to the other, mimicking the movements the world had seen a million times in the dance video. She had rhythm. She had style.

And she had his full attention.

There was no doubt about it. His blood was definitely flowing through his body a little quicker now. This emergency mission had just got a whole lot more interesting.

Something sparked in his brain. Recognition. He could practically feel the hormones surge through his body. He couldn't stop the smile dancing around the edges of his lips. For the first time in a long time there was a spark. A something. If he could grab this sensation right now and bottle it, he would.

Who was she again? He filtered through the names Gibbs had given him. Gabrielle somebody? Although he'd been with Doctors Without Borders for three years, it was impossible to meet everyone. There were thirty thousand staff covering seventy countries. They saved lives by providing medical aid where it was needed most—armed conflicts, epidemics, natural disasters, and other crisis situations. There were also longer-term projects designed to tackle health crises and support people who couldn't otherwise access health care. Every day was different. He'd just spent three months covering a burns unit. The mission before that had been in Haiti, offering free surgery. The time before that had been in a DWB hospital in Syria, dealing mainly with paediatrics.

She lifted her hands above her head, giving him a better glimpse of the indentation of her waist and swell of her hips in those shorts. He couldn't help but smile. This girl knew how to dance.

If he'd seen her in a club he would have been mesmerised. Her hips sashayed to the music. Her head flicked from side to side. Her whole body was bouncing. If they'd been in a club, he might even have fought the temptation to step up behind her, press his body against hers and join in. But they weren't in a club. They were in the middle of the Narumba jungle.

Her feet crossed in the clunky boots and she

spun around. It was obviously meant to be a full circle, but she caught sight of the unfamiliar figure and stumbled midway.

His actions were automatic. He stepped forward and caught her elbow before she landed on the floor, pulling her up against him.

Her eyes were wide. Her skin soft. And the scent of roses drifted up around him. The hand that had shot out to break her fall had landed on his chest as he'd grabbed her.

For a second they were frozen in time. The music was pumping around them, the heat of the jungle rising between them, and the darkness of the night enveloping everything.

Her eyes were the darkest brown he'd ever seen. They suited her tanned skin and chocolate hair. It was only a split second, but the heat from the palm of her hand seemed to penetrate through his thin T-shirt straight to the skin on his chest. He sucked in a breath just as she stepped backwards.

'Gabrielle?'

As if the stranger standing in front of her, looking like film-star material, wasn't enough, the deep throaty voice sent a shudder of electrical pulses flooding through her system that started in the palm of her hand and shot a direct route to her fluttering heart.

It took a second to catch her breath again.

No, it took more than a second.

Darn it. He was smiling at her. A perfect straight-white-teeth kind of smile.

Her palm was tingling from where she'd made contact with the firm muscles on his chest. He was tall, lean and wide. She'd bet every part of him was as muscled as his chest.

He had a buzz cut—like someone from the army. In fact, she'd put money on it that he'd served in the military. He had that demeanour about him, that aura of confidence as he stood there in his khaki army-style trousers and a thin dark green T-shirt.

He held his hand out to her again. 'May I have this dance?' he joked.

She gave an inward shudder as her brain kicked into gear. She spun to turn the music down on her speakers. What must she look like?

In this area she spent twelve hours with clothes fastened up to her neck, not even revealing a glimpse of her ankles. By the time she got back to camp she needed an instant shower, a quick feed and clothes she could relax in.

She took a deep breath and turned around, regaining her composure and putting her game face into place.

She shook his hand and smiled. 'Yes, I'm Gabrielle. But you have me at a disadvantage. We haven't met before.'

He frowned. 'You haven't heard from Gibbs?'

She nodded and put her hand on her hips. 'Oh, I heard.' She lifted her hands in the air and made quotation marks, 'You girls can't stay there by yourselves. I'll find you someone.' She tilted her head to the side. 'I'm assuming you're the some-one.'

He glanced around the tent as if he were sizing up the place. Then, in a move that only reinforced what she was thinking, he turned and looked out-side at the camp, checking out the surroundings. Once he seemed satisfied he turned back to her. 'I guess I am. I'm Sullivan Darcy.'

She couldn't hide her smile. 'Gibbs has sent me my own Mr Darcy?'

He raised his eyebrows as she continued. The accent was unmistakable. 'US army?'

He nodded. 'I was. Now I'm with Doctors Without Borders.'

She walked over to a table and lifted some pa-perwork. 'What's your speciality? Medicine? In-fectious diseases?'

He pulled a face. 'You'll hate this.'

Her stomach clenched. 'Why?'

'I'm a surgeon.'

'Oh.' Her stomach sank like a stone. In some circumstances a surgeon would be great but it was not exactly what she needed right now. She bit her bottom lip, trying to find the right words.

He stepped forward. 'But if it helps I did a refresher and read all the protocols on the trip here. Just give me some instructions and a prescribing regime and I'm all yours.'

He held out his hands as if he were inviting her to step into them. For the first time in for ever the thought actually did cross her mind.

Missions were exhausting, the time off in between short and frantic. She couldn't remember the last time she'd felt a buzz when she'd met someone. A connection. The chance to tease, the chance to flirt.

Her own Mr Darcy was pretty much looking like manna from heaven right now.

She was lucky. She'd never had the same pressure her brother had—to find the perfect partner, settle down, marry and get ready to run a country.

Sixteen years of being in the spotlight as the perfect princess in Mirinez had been enough. Medicine had been considered an 'honourable' profession and she'd climbed on that plane to study medicine at Cambridge University, breathing a huge sigh of relief. Since then she'd only returned for weddings, funerals and a few state events. Mirinez had lost interest in her. She hadn't been in press reports for years. And that was exactly the way she wanted it to stay.

His green eyes met hers again. 'That accent? French?'

She shrugged. 'Close enough.'

She pulled out a chair at the table and gestured for him to sit down before he quizzed her any further. 'Let's focus on what needs to get done in the next two weeks.'

She shot him a smile. He stepped closer. His chest was barely inches from her nose and she caught a whiff of pure pheromones. Oh, she could pretty it up by saying it was a combination of soap, remnants of musk antiperspirant and some subtle cologne, but from the effect it was having on her senses it felt like one hundred per cent testosterone.

He didn't seem worried about their closeness. In fact, she could almost bet that he thrived on it. The thin fabric covering his broad chest brushed against her arm as he sat down. 'Like I said, tell me what you need and I'm your guy.'

She pushed away the rush of thoughts that flooded her brain as she pulled forward a map. She circled areas for him. 'We've done here, here and here. In the next two weeks we need to cover this area, and north of the river. We expect to see around seven hundred people a day.'

She was glad that he didn't flinch at the volume of people who still needed to be seen.

He reached over to study the map. 'How do you work your clinics?'

She gave a nod as the hairs on his arms brushed against her. *Yip.*

'The TB regime is harsh. We split our duties. We have two nurses, a few local volunteers...' she frowned '...and only one translator.'

He waved his hand. 'Don't worry about that. My Farsi is passable. The dialect might be a little different from where I've been working but I'm sure I'll muddle through.'

Muddle through. She smiled. It was like something her grandmother used to say in private. Not quite the expression she'd expected from the muscular guy who screamed 'army'.

'You're good with languages?'

He looked amused. 'You're surprised?' There was a challenge in his words and a glint in his green eyes.

Her brain couldn't quite find the words.

He gave a little nod. 'I speak ten languages.'

She blinked. 'Ten?'

He shrugged. 'I was a navy brat. I moved around a lot. I picked up languages easily. It was the only way to fit in.'

She pressed her lips together then rearranged the papers.

Interesting. It was clear he'd hit a sore spot.

She got straight to the point. 'Lucy and Estelle deal mainly with the patients who require treatment for their TB. Gretchen dispenses the medicines. The volunteers administer and read the tests.'

He raised his eyebrows and she quickly reassured him. 'We train them ourselves.'

She opened a laptop. A spreadsheet appeared on the screen. She licked her lips. He was watching her closely. It was a little unnerving. 'We're estimating sixty per cent of the population have TB in one form or another. Some are active, some are latent, and some...' she sighed '...are multi-resistant.'

'How many?'

She nodded slowly. He must have read at least some of the information that Gibbs had sent to him. She let out a sigh. 'Around twelve per cent.'

'That high?' He couldn't hide his surprise. He'd known that drug resistance was rising all around the world, but the figure was higher than he expected.

'Tell me what you need me to do.' He was unnerved. And Sullivan Darcy wasn't used to feeling unnerved. He was used to being the expert in the field. He was used to knowing his subject area inside out. And as Gabrielle's rose-hinted scent wound its way around him he needed to find some focus.

Gabrielle nodded and licked those pink lips

again. She pulled open a drawer next to her and pulled out some kind of cool pack. He watched as she unwrapped it and pulled out the biggest bar of chocolate he'd ever seen.

She gave him a cheeky smile. 'I hate mushy chocolate.' She broke off a piece and handed it to him. He automatically reached out and took it.

'I didn't peg you as a chocoholic.'

She shrugged, her brown eyes gleaming in the artificial light in the tent. 'I have lots of secrets, you'll just need to hang around to find them out.'

He almost choked on the chocolate he'd just put in his mouth. It was almost a direct invitation.

He leaned back in the chair, stretching one arm out to press the button to restart the music. 'I can see Justin and I are going to become very good friends.'

He folded his arms across his chest and smiled.

CHAPTER TWO

GABRIELLE NORMALLY SLEPT like the dead. It was a skill she'd developed over the last six years of working for Doctors Without Borders. An essential skill. No one needed an overtired, grumpy medic.

But she'd been awake since four-thirty. She'd watched the sun rise as she'd contemplated some more chocolate, wishing she'd had a secret stash of wine.

She could swear she could almost hear him breathing in the tent next to hers. This wasn't normal. It couldn't be normal.

Most men she'd met in her life had fulfilled a purpose. She always chose carefully. No one who would sell stories to the press. No one who was secretly looking for a princess. Guys who were interested in relatively short-term gigs. Six months maximum. Enough time for some getting-to-know-you, some trust and some intimacy. But no promises, no intentions and no time for the petty squabbles and fights to set in. She'd always been the one in control.

She'd never actually felt that *whoosh* when

she'd met someone. More like a flirtatious curiosity.

But with Sullivan Darcy it wasn't just a whoosh. It was a full-blown tornado. For a woman who was always used to being in control, it was more than a little unnerving.

And she was mad with herself. Being caught dancing by him had thrown her off her usually professional stride. Gibbs hadn't told her anything about the doctor coming to work with her and last night it had seemed too forward to pry.

He'd said he was a navy brat. What exactly did he mean? The guy could speak ten languages? Really? It kind of stuck in her throat. Languages had been one of her major failures as a royal. Mirinez bordered three countries, France, Italy and Monaco. Her native language was French. English had been instilled in her as a child and spending her university years and training time in the UK had served her well.

At a push she could stammer a few words in a few other languages. The same standard statements required by doctors. *I'm a doctor, can I help? Are you in pain? What's your name?* But that was it. Languages had always been her Achilles' heel.

She'd spent her life being top of all her other classes. Her brother, Andreas, had consistently been annoyed that his younger sister could out do him in every academic subject.

And being a doctor was kind of a strange thing. She'd worked with plenty of other doctors who were experts in their fields—just like she was in hers. But she'd never really met a guy who seemed smarter than her.

Mr Ten Languages felt like a little bit of a threat. It was making her stomach curl in all kinds of strange ways. She wasn't quite sure if it was pure and utter attraction or a tiny bit of jealousy.

She flipped open her laptop to check the list of patients for today. Her emails blinked up. Three hundred and seventy-six. She'd read them all soon. The sixteen-hour shifts here were all-consuming. By the time they got back to camp, washed up and had some food, she didn't have much energy left. Reviewing patient details and stock supplies was a must. Reading hundreds of emails when a large percentage of them were probably spam? That could wait.

She ran her eyes down the list. The work was never-ending. TB was a relentless disease. There was no quick fix here.

'All set.' Gretchen, the pharmacist, appeared at the entrance to the tent with a smile on her face. 'I've just met our new doc.' She winked at Gabrielle. 'In some parts of Switzerland, we would call him eye candy.'

Gabrielle burst out laughing at Gretchen's turn of phrase. They'd worked together for Doctors Without Borders for the last six years—always on the TB programmes. It had been Gabrielle's first official diagnosis of a patient when she'd been a medical student and had been her passion ever since.

'I don't know what you mean.' She smiled in return. 'I'm far too busy working to contemplate any kind of candy.'

Gretchen wagged her finger at her. 'Don't think I don't know about the hidden candy.' She raised her eyebrows. 'Maybe it's time to contemplate another kind.'

'Gretchen!' The woman ducked as Gabrielle flung a ball of paper at her.

There was a deep laugh and Sullivan appeared with the crushed ball in his hand. 'Anything I should know about?'

She could feel the heat rush into her cheeks. It was like being a teenager all over again. She stood up quickly, grabbing the laptop and her backpack. 'Not at all. Let's go, Dr Darcy, time to learn some new skills.'

She was baiting him and she could tell he knew it. He shook his head and slung his own backpack over his shoulder. 'I like to learn something new every day.'

He wasn't joking. And Gabrielle took him at his word.

As soon as they'd travelled to their first stop and set up, she took him aside. 'You know the drill. Ordinary TB is horrible enough. It kills one point four million people every year with another nine million suffering from the disease, mainly in developing countries like Narumba. Along with malaria and HIV it's one of the three main killer infectious diseases. Drug resistance and multi-drug-resistant TB numbers are increasing all the time. Because it's spread through the air when people cough and sneeze, it's virtually impossible to stop the spread. One third of the world's population is infected with mycobacterium tuberculosis but it's dormant in their bodies. Ten per cent of these people will develop active TB at some point in their life.'

There was passion and enthusiasm in her voice. There was also a hint of anger. She was angry at what this disease was being allowed to do to people all around the world. He liked that about her.

'We've been using the same archaic test for the last one hundred and twenty years and the test is only accurate half of the time—even less so if the patient has HIV. I hope you're comfortable with kids. We have a new test for TB but it's not suitable for kids. They need the traditional test and we have the facility for chest X-rays if necessary. Mainly, we go on clinical presentation and history.'

He nodded. He'd read more notes after Gabrielle had gone to bed. He was happy to do something to pass yet another long night when he couldn't sleep.

She kept talking, her voice going at a hundred miles an hour. 'You know the clinical presentation, don't you? A persistent cough, fever, weight loss, chest pain and breathlessness. The nurses will bring through anyone who has tested positive and is showing resistance to rifampicin. You'll need to check them over clinically before starting their prescription.' She pointed to a printed algorithm. 'We have a chart for adults and a chart for paeds. The new test also doesn't show anyone who has non-pulmonary TB. The nurses will bring through anyone with a history who gives concern.'

He blinked as he looked at the clinic list. 'You see this many patients every day?'

She nodded, her brown hair bouncing. It was tied up on her head again. She was wearing a high-necked, long-sleeved shirt and long trousers, even though the temperature was soaring. He was lucky. He had on shorts and a T-shirt, but even so the heat was causing trickles of sweat to run down between his shoulder blades.

She gave a little tug at her neck. 'Okay?' he queried.

She gave a nod. 'Let's just get started. We need to see as many patients as we can.'

She wasn't joking. It was only seven a.m., but news of their clinic must have spread because there was already a queue forming outside.

Four hours later he'd seen more kids in this TB clinic than he'd ever want to. Doctors Without Borders might be there to try and tackle the TB epidemic, but to the people of Narumba he was just a doctor. His surgical highlight of his day so far had been grabbing some equipment and a scalpel to drain a few abscesses. He'd also seen a huge variety of skin conditions, variations of asthma, diabetes, polio and sleeping sickness. He'd seen multiple patients with HIV—mixed with TB it would be deadly for many of the people he'd seen today. He could barely keep track of how many patients he'd actually seen. And the queue outside? It just kept getting longer and longer.

Long queues were good. He had never been work shy. Long days were much more preferable to long nights. If he exhausted himself with work, he might actually get a few hours' sleep tonight.

He kept a smile on his face as another mother came in, clutching her child to her chest.

He nodded towards her, speaking in Narumbi. 'I'm Dr Darcy, one of the team. What's your name, and your son's name?'

She gave an anxious smile at his good grasp of the language. 'I'm Chiari. This is Alum, he's sick.'

Sullivan nodded and held out his hands to take the little boy. 'How old is he?'

'Four,' she answered quickly.

He blinked. The little boy resembled a two-year-old. The weight loss of TB had clearly affected him. He took out his stethoscope and gently sounded the boy's chest. The rattle was clear and he had the swollen and tender lymph nodes around his neck. He asked a few more questions. 'Does anyone else in the family have symptoms?'

The woman's face tightened. 'My husband died last month.'

He nodded in sympathy. There was a little pang in his chest. He recognised the expression in her eyes. He'd seen that loss reflected in his own eyes often enough when he looked in the mirror. But there was no time for that here. He had a job to do.

'What about you? Have you been tested?'

She shook her head and looked anxiously at

her son. 'I don't have time to be tested. I need to take care of Alum.'

Sullivan reached over and put his hand on her arm.

'I understand. I do. I'm sorry for your loss. We need to make sure that you are well enough to take care of Alum. We can treat you both at the same time.' He glanced outside the tent. 'I can get one of the nurses to do the test. It's a new kind. Your results will be available in a few hours. We can start you both on treatment immediately.'

He sent a silent prayer upwards, hoping that her test didn't show multi-resistant TB. Chances were if she had it, her son had it too. Normal TB took a minimum of six months to treat. But if Chiari showed signs of resistance to rifampicin and isoniazid she'd be considered to have MDR-TB. The MDR-TB drug regime was an arduous eight months of painful injections and more than ten thousand pills, taking two years to complete. The side effects could be severe— permanent hearing loss, psychosis, nausea, skin rashes and renal failure had all been reported. But the worse news was there was only a forty-eight per cent cure rate.

He pressed again. 'What about Alum? Has he been eating? Has he had night sweats or lost weight?'

Chiari nodded slowly. He could see the weariness in her eyes that was obviously felt in her heart. She'd likely just nursed her husband through this disease. Now there was a chance she could have it herself, and have to nurse her son through it too.

He stood up, holding Alum in his arms. 'Let's go and see one of our nurses. I'd like to try and give Alum some medicine to help with his weight loss, and start some medicine for TB. Our pharmacist, Gretchen, will give you the medicines and teach you how to give them to Alum. Then we can arrange to get your test done.'

After a few moments of contemplation Chiari stood up and nodded. Sullivan carried the little boy into the next tent. The nurses Lucy and Estelle nodded towards a few chairs in the corner. This was the fiftieth child he'd taken through to them this morning. They knew exactly what to do.

He filled out the electronic prescription for Gretchen and left her to explain to Chiari how to dispense the medicines for Alum. The reality was that children had to take adult pills, split or crushed. There were no TB medicines ready for kids in the field.

Gabrielle appeared at his side. 'Everything okay?' Her hand touched his shoulder.

He reached up automatically and his hand covered hers. He appreciated the thought. She was looking out for him. He met her dark brown eyes. 'It's a steep learning curve.'

She looked a little surprised. 'I thought it would only take someone like you an hour to ace.'

Was she joking with him again? He shook his head. 'Maybe after the two weeks. But not on the first day.'

She tilted her head to the side. 'I heard you talking there. You really do have a good grasp of the language. How do you do that?'

'It's similar to Farsi. It was a necessary skill when I was in the army. We treated a lot of civilians as well as servicemen. It doesn't matter where you are in life—or what you do—communication is always the key.'

She gave a careful nod. He folded his arms across his chest. 'There are a few cases we might need to chat about later. Adults. They're being tested but I'm almost sure that both of them are non-pulmonary TB.'

He could tell she was trying her best not to look surprised. Non-pulmonary TB was the hardest catch. The normal test didn't work, neither did a chest X-ray. There were so many variations that the symptoms were often mistaken for something else.

'No problem. If you give me the notes I'll check them over.'

He picked up the two sets of notes he'd started

to write, his hand brushing against hers as she reached for them. 'Actually,' he said, 'I'd kind of like to be there to see what you think. Let's just call it part of the learning curve.'

The edges of her lips turned upwards. She really was cute when she smiled.

'You want a teaching session?' There was a definite glint in her eye. He leaned forward a little. He could think of a whole host of things that Gabrielle could teach him.

She was close. She was so close that he could glimpse a few little freckles across the bridge of her nose. Her brown eyes were darker than any he'd seen before and fringed with long dark lashes. It was clear she wasn't wearing any make-up—but she didn't need it. He could quite happily look at that face all day.

'Sullivan?' She nudged him with her elbow.

He started. 'Sorry, what?'

Her smile spread. She raised her eyebrows. 'You were staring.'

It was a statement that sounded like a bit of a satisfied accusation. Nothing could dampen the sparks that were flying between them.

He could feel them. She could feel them. He'd been here less than twenty-four hours. How on earth would he manage a whole two weeks around a woman like Gabrielle Cartier?

He was still getting over the wonder of actually feeling…*something* again. There had been a number of women over the last three years—but no relationships. He wasn't in a relationship kind of place. But now he could feel the buzz in the air. It felt alive around him, pulling him from the fog he'd been in. Gabrielle Cartier was like the freshest air that had swept over his skin in the last three years.

Two weeks could be perfect. It was just long enough to be familiar with someone but not long enough for any expectations.

He smiled back. 'I wasn't staring.'

'Yes, you were.'

He nudged her back. 'I wasn't. I was contemplating life.'

She laughed. 'I don't even want to take a guess at what that means.'

She was right. She didn't. But he couldn't stop staring at that smile.

She glanced at the notes. 'How about we see these two patients now? It doesn't really work well if the two doctors are seeing patients together.' She took a hesitant breath. 'We just have too many patients.'

He nodded carefully. 'I get it, you don't like having to teach the rookie.' He shrugged. 'Ten minutes. That's all. Then hopefully I won't need to ask for a second opinion again. I'll be confident to make the diagnosis myself.'

He wasn't joking. He would be confident. Sullivan had never needed to be shown anything twice in his whole career. He'd embraced the doctor's motto of see one, do one, teach one.

Gabrielle's gaze narrowed a little. She gave a quick nod. 'No problem.'

The next few days passed quickly. Every time she turned, Sullivan Darcy was at her back. Or maybe it just seemed like that.

He hadn't exaggerated. He picked up things quickly. He'd diagnosed more patients with non-pulmonary TB. He'd adjusted antibiotic regimes for patients who were struggling with side effects. He'd spent hours and hours with patients with the dual diagnosis of HIV and TB.

His only tiny flash of frustration had been with a young child who was suffering from appendicitis. They had no real surgical equipment in the field. No theatre. No way to sterilise the tools that would be needed for surgery.

The nearest hospital was four hours away across a dry and bumpy road. Finding transport was a problem. All they could do was give the child some pain relief and a shot of antibiotics in the hope it would stave off any potential complications before sending him off in the back of a worn-out jeep. As the jeep disappeared into the distance Sullivan kicked an empty water canister clean across the camp, his hands balled tightly into fists.

She watched from a distance.

There was something about him that was so intriguing. Ask him anything medical and he could talk for ever. Ask about training placements, hospitals, work colleagues and experiences with Doctors Without Borders and he'd happily share all his experiences.

But ask about his time in the army or his family and he became tight-lipped. And there was something else Gabrielle had noticed about Sullivan Darcy.

He had the same skill that she'd developed over the years—the art of changing the subject. She'd recognised it instantly. And it intrigued her.

Had he noticed the same skill in her?

It was late. The sun was starting to set in the sky. They'd stayed much later at this site. It was one of the furthest away from their camp—which meant that the people in this area rarely saw medical staff. It made sense to do as much as they possibly could while they were there.

There was a noise to her left and she looked up. The heat of the day rarely dissipated and she'd undone the first few buttons on her shirt and pulled it out from her trousers. One of the tribal leaders had emerged from behind some scrub trees and was scowling at her.

There were a few other men behind him, all talking rapidly and gesturing towards her.

She glanced around. Lucy and Gretchen were nowhere in sight. Estelle was at the other end of the site, loading their transport. In the dim light it was difficult to see anyone else. Their local translator had already left.

The tribal leader strode towards her, gesturing and talking loudly. She'd almost baulked when Gibbs had refused to leave the female staff alone on the mission. But the truth was there had been a few incidents when a traditional tribal leader had refused to allow the women access to their tribes.

It had only happened twice. But Asfar Modarres had played a vital role in negotiating access to the people suffering from TB.

The tribal leader marched straight up to her face, his voice getting louder by the second. She quickly started tucking her shirt back in. No skin around her waist had been on display, but it was clear that something was making him unhappy.

The rest of the men crowded behind the leader. She swallowed. Her mouth was instantly dry.

In the distance she could see Estelle's head jerk up, but Estelle was too far away to offer any immediate assistance. Gabrielle had never been a woman who was easily intimidated. But she'd never been crowded by a group of angry men. The others had started to fan out behind their leader, surrounding her on all sides. Her automatic reaction was to start to step backwards, trying to maintain some distance between her and them.

Any Narumbi words that she'd picked up from the interpreter flew from her brain. 'I'm a doctor. Wh-what do you want?' She could only stammer in English.

The tribal leader poked her in the shoulder with one finger. It wasn't a violent action. But that one firm poke was enough to make her stumble over her own feet and thump down onto the ground, a cloud of red dust puffing around her.

The noise came from behind. It wasn't a shout. It was a roar. She recognised Sullivan's voice instantly, although she had no idea what he'd just said in Narumbi.

All the men looked up immediately. She could hear the thuds and a few seconds later the men were pushed roughly aside, several landing in the dust like she had.

Strong hands pulled her up roughly. She hadn't even had time to catch her breath. One arm wrapped tightly around her shoulder, pulling her close against his rigid muscles. The words were flowing from his mouth in fury.

She didn't have a clue what Sullivan was saying, but it was clear that the men could understand every single syllable. The tribal leader looked annoyed for a few seconds and tried to answer back. But he was stopped by the palm of Sullivan's hand held inches from his face.

Sullivan's voice lowered. The tone changed. Became threatening. A kind of don't-even-think-about-it message emanating from every pore in his body. She could feel the vibrations coming from his chest, shoulders and arms. But Sullivan wasn't shaking through fear or intimidation. She knew straight away he was shaking with rage.

It was a whole new side of him. She'd seen the cheeky side. She'd even seen the flirtatious side. She'd seen the professional side, his willingness to adapt to a situation outside his normal expertise and practise effectively.

Now she was seeing something else entirely. This was the man who'd served in the military. This was the man who left her in no doubt about how vested he was in protecting the people he worked with. Part of her had felt a little resentful when Gibbs had told her he was sending a man to work with them. Right now, she'd never been so glad that Sullivan Darcy was right by her side.

The palm of Sullivan's hand hadn't moved. He was still speaking in his low, dangerously controlled voice.

The men exchanged nervous glances. It didn't seem to matter that Sullivan was outnumbered.

His tall, muscular frame and no-nonsense approach left no one in doubt about his potential.

The tribal leader shook his head and muttered, casting a sideways glance at Gabrielle again. After what seemed like an endless silence—but must only have been a few seconds—he spun around, his cloak wide as he stamped back off into the scrub.

Her chest was tight. She hadn't even realised she was holding her breath until Sullivan released the firm grip on her shoulders and blocked her line of vision.

She jolted and gave a shudder. Sullivan crouched down, his face parallel with hers. 'Gabrielle, are you okay? Did they hurt you?'

His hands were on her, pushing up the sleeve of her shirt, checking first one arm and then the other. He knelt down, reaching for her trouser leg.

She grabbed his hand. 'Stop it. Don't.'

Every muscle in her body was tense, every hair on her skin standing on end.

His dark green eyes met hers and she saw a flash of understanding. She was still gripping him tightly, her knuckles turning white.

He put his other hand over hers and rubbed gently. It was comforting—reassuring. The thud of other footsteps sounded. It was Estelle, quickly followed by Lucy and Gretchen. 'Gabrielle? What happened? Did they hurt you?'

She could hear the panic in their voices.

Her eyes were fixed on Sullivan's hand rubbing hers. A warm feeling was starting to spread up her arm. She sucked in a deep breath, filling her lungs and trying to clear her head.

Sullivan seemed to sense the tension leaving her body. He kept hold of her hand but straightened up, glancing around at the other women.

'Have you finished packing up? I think it would be a good idea to make the journey back to camp now. It was a misunderstanding. A language thing. He misunderstood something that Gabrielle had told his wife. He was unhappy and was angry when he realised she couldn't speak Narumbi. We've done all we can do here today. I'll need to file a report.'

Gabrielle licked her dry lips. She was the leader of this expedition. The decision when to pack up and go back to camp had always been hers. Normally, she would be offended but this time she didn't feel slighted at all. She just wanted a chance to get back to camp and take stock.

'We're ready,' said Gretchen quickly. 'I'll drive.'

She was decisive. Gabrielle gave a nod and walked over to where her backpack and laptop were. The rest of the staff spoke quietly to each other as she climbed into the back seat of their custom jeep. She wasn't surprised when Sullivan climbed in next to her.

She waited until the engine had been started and the barren countryside started to rush past. 'What did you say to them? What had I done to upset him? What did I say to his wife?' she asked quietly. She wasn't looking at him. She wasn't sure that she could. She fixed her eyes on the horizon. Thoughts of the language barrier were spinning around in her head. She hated it that she hadn't understood a single word out there. It had made her feel like a complete and utter failure.

Sullivan reached over and put his hand on her leg. Some people might think it was too forward an action but somehow she knew it was only an act of reassurance. 'He was unhappy because his wife had told him you'd given her a different medicine for the wound on her leg. She'd been using something that his mother made—some kind of paste. You said she had an infection and needed antibiotics.'

'That was it?' She was frustrated beyond belief. 'That woman had a serious infection in her lower leg. If I hadn't treated it, there's a chance she could lose her leg.' She replayed events over in her head. The consultation with the woman. The altercation between Sullivan and the tribal leader.

He pressed his lips together. 'I said exactly

what I should say. I told them their behaviour was shameful. We were there to help them and everyone in their tribe. I told them if the women around me didn't feel safe, we wouldn't be back.'

This time she did turn her head and narrow her gaze. He looked her straight in the eye.

'Is that your poker face?'

He frowned. 'What?'

'Is that your poker face? I might not speak Narumbi, but I don't think that's exactly what you said,' she replied carefully.

His steady gaze hadn't wavered. He was good at this. She'd have to remember that.

He licked his lips, his first tiny sign of a release of tension.

'Then it's just as well you aren't fluent in Narumbi,' he said promptly.

He lowered his voice. 'I won't allow you—any of you—to be treated like that.' He sighed. 'I understand that we're in a different country. A different culture means different people. I respect their views. But if they're hostile towards you, or threaten you...' He squeezed her thigh and looked her straight in the eye. Last time she'd been this close they'd been alone in the tent when he'd arrived. The light had been much dimmer. This time she could see the intensity of the deep green of his eyes dotted with tiny flecks of gold. '...I'd fight to the death,' he finished.

She gulped. He meant it. She didn't doubt for a second that he absolutely meant it. 'Thank you,' she whispered as she shifted in her seat. How come he could look at her unflinchingly one second and tell her only a version of the truth, then the next the sincerity in his eyes could take her breath away?

She looked down at her hands. 'I hate not being in control,' she said quietly. 'I hate the fact that things can slip so fast, so quickly.' She shook her head. 'If I could have spoken the language I could have explained.' She tugged at her shirt. 'Or maybe he didn't like my clothes.'

'Stop it.' His voice was firm. 'Gabrielle, you and the rest of the women in the team are appropriately dressed. His mother is the head woman in their tribe. He thinks you insulted her expertise.' He put his hand on his chest. 'It's a different culture. Women in their tribe aren't really treated with much respect. Maybe that bothers him? Maybe he's more modern than he seems—so the thought that someone questions the respect his mother holds made him angry.'

He leaned forward and touched her cheek. 'You made a clinical decision. You're a good doctor, Gabrielle. If you hadn't given his wife antibiotics it's likely she would lose her leg. And I've told him that. In no uncertain terms. Give yourself a break. Their behaviour was unreasonable.'

He settled back into his seat and folded his arms. 'And I told them that too.'

For the first time since it had happened she gave a small smile. 'And a whole lot more too.'

She saw him suck in a deep breath. His gaze hadn't faltered from hers, but she could tell he was contemplating his words.

'I've grown a little fond of you. I'd hate anything to happen on my watch.'

She felt a prickle go down her spine. Was this good or bad?

Part of her wanted to smile. It was almost an acknowledgement of the mutual attraction between them. But part of it sounded a bit over-protective. Sullivan couldn't know, but she'd deliberately left that part of her life behind. Being a doctor and working away from Mirinez gave her the freedom she'd never experienced as a child. It wasn't like Mirinez was some kind of superpower. It was a small country but prosperous—mainly due to its tax haven status. But her great-grandmother had been a film star, which had put Mirinez firmly on the media map.

She glanced at the others in the jeep. Estelle, Lucy and Gretchen were chatting amongst themselves in the front. They weren't listening to Sullivan and Gabrielle's conversation at all. The jeep had moved quickly. Even though the road was bumpy they were far away from the site of the camp today. What's more, she felt safe around Sullivan. Now he was sitting right next to her she finally felt as if she could relax. She bit her lip. 'Well, I might have grown fond of you too, but I'm not your responsibility, Sullivan.'

He only smiled. That was the annoying part of him. That darned confidence. Over the last three years she'd found it common amongst the medics who'd served in the army. Maybe she was even a little envious of it. She had felt vulnerable today—and she hated that.

'I'll take that under advisement,' said Sullivan smartly. He leaned forward and whispered, 'We've only got another week to go. Then it's back to base. How long have you got before you're back on another mission?'

There was an intense twinkle in his eye. He'd already admitted he was fond of her. Headquarters were back in Paris. All staff that arrived back had a few days debrief, then, unless people were rushing back to see their families, there was usually a few days where they would let their hair down before everyone dispersed to their next mission.

She licked her lips. 'I might have around ten days. I'm not sure where I'm going next. Gibbs hasn't told me yet. What about you?'

Mad thoughts were already flashing through

her head. Ten days in Paris with Sullivan Darcy? Now, that could be fun.

He raised his eyebrows. 'I haven't committed yet.'

'You haven't?' She was surprised.

He shook his head. 'I have a few things I should really take care of back home.'

She straightened up. 'What kind of things?' He'd never mentioned a family back home. And he'd been flirting with her. Just like she'd been flirting back. He didn't wear a ring. But if he suddenly mentioned a Mrs Darcy he would see a whole new side of Gabrielle Cartier. She just wasn't that kind of girl.

He let out a long slow breath and looked away. 'I really should take care of my father's house. He died a few years ago and I've been too busy working to get around to clearing it out and sorting through his things.'

She hoped her sigh of relief wasn't as noticeable as it felt. 'Who takes care of it now?'

He grimaced. 'No one really. I've only been back for a few odd days at a time. I have someone take care of the garden, and I've made sure that the services continue to be paid. But at the moment it's really just collecting dust.'

The tone of his voice had changed. It didn't have the strength of earlier, or the cheekiness that she'd heard on other occasions. There was some-

thing wistful about his tone. Even a little regret-
ful. It was a side of Sullivan Darcy she hadn't
seen before.

This time she made the move. She reached over
and put her hand over his. 'Maybe you needed
to let it collect dust for a while. You have to wait
until you're ready to do things. That time might
be now.'

For a second she thought he might come back
with a usual cheeky quip, but something flashed
across his eyes and he stared at her hand covering his.

He gave a slow nod. 'You could be right.' Then
one eyebrow rose. 'But I don't want you to make a
habit of it. I get the impression if you think you're
right all the time you could be unbearable.'

She couldn't help but grin. This was how he
wanted to play it. It seemed Dr Darcy could reveal
the tiniest element of himself before his shutters
came down again.

She could appreciate that. Particularly in an
environment like this when things could flare
up at any second and you had to be ready for any
kind of emergency.

He leaned towards her again, this time so close
that his stubble brushed against her cheek. 'Trouble is,' he whispered in her ear, 'what can we possibly do to get through the next week?'

A red-hot flush flooded through her body. She

tried not to look at the muscled pecs visibly outlined by his thin T-shirt, or the biceps clearly defined by his folded arms. Sullivan Darcy was one sexy guy. But two could play that game.

She moved, stretching her back out then straightening her shirt, allowing the fabric to tighten over her breasts.

Then she gave him a playful smile. 'Who knows, Dr Darcy? I guess we'll just need to think of something.'

CHAPTER THREE

FOR THE LAST few days they'd danced around each other. It was ridiculous. And Sullivan knew it. They were both grown adults and could do whatever they wanted to.

But he got the definite feeling that although Gabrielle was attracted to him as much as he was to her, she wasn't comfortable about initiating a relationship under the microscopic view of their colleagues.

And she was right. It wouldn't really be professional. No matter how much his brain told him otherwise in the depths of the pitch-black nights in Narumba.

He'd been furious when he'd seen those men around her. That leader *attacking* her. Anytime he thought about it for too long he felt his rage re-ignite. As soon as they'd got back to camp he'd contacted Gibbs and filed a report. Another team would replace them as soon as they left. He wanted to make sure precautions were taken to safeguard the staff.

Then he'd written another note, asking the staff to try and check on Alum and Chiari to see how they were coping with the medicine regime, and if they were having any side effects, and yet another about the tribal leader's wife, asking someone to check on her leg and her antibiotics.

It didn't matter where they pitched up. The clinics were packed every day and he saw a hundred variations of Alum and Chiari. That, mixed in with a hundred children who'd been orphaned and a hundred parents who'd nursed their children through their last days made him realise it might be time to have a break.

He'd never contemplated one before. Never wanted to. But the desperate situation of some of these families was beginning to get to him.

He wasn't quite sure why he'd told Gabrielle about the reason he hadn't signed up yet for another mission. Maybe she'd just asked at the right moment.

Or maybe he was just distracted by the possibility of ten days in Paris with a woman who was slowly but surely driving him crazy. If he didn't taste those pink lips soon he might just decide to set up his own camp inside her tent.

Every night when they got back, she showered, changed into one of a variety of coloured T-shirts and usually those darn shorts. There should be a licence against them.

The *whoosh* he'd felt when he'd first seen her was turning into a full-blown tornado. Maybe it was just the blow-out of actually feeling something again. Maybe, after three years, his head was rising above the parapet a bit. He'd met a few women in the last three years but he'd been going through the motions. There had been no emotion involved, just a pure male hormonal response. Gabrielle was different. Gabrielle had an aura around her. A buzz. He smiled to himself. She was like one of those ancient sirens who had lured sailors to their deaths. He'd have to remember not to let her sing. Or talk. Or dance. Or wear those shorts.

It didn't matter that they were the only five people in the camp. It didn't matter that he was the only male for miles. As soon as he heard the music start to play in her tent he was drawn like a moth to the flame.

Gabrielle could conduct whole conversations while she sashayed around to the beat of the music. He'd recognised it was her *thing*. Her down time. So far they'd discussed fourteen special patient cases, numerous plans for the next day's camps, treatment regimes, transfer times and some testing issues.

It was hard to have a conversation when the best pair of legs he'd ever seen was on display.

And tonight was no different from any other—with the exception of the soul music. She smiled as he appeared at the tent entrance. 'Lionel and

Luther tonight,' she said as her loose hair bounced around. 'Decided it was time for a change.'

He nodded as he moved towards her. She'd tied a red T-shirt in a knot at her waist but hadn't got around to tying her hair up on her head as normal. It was longer than he'd realised, with a natural curl at the ends.

Sullivan wasn't usually a dancer. It wasn't that he couldn't feel the beat of the music, it was just that he'd never felt the urge to rave in a dark disco. And he certainly hadn't felt the urge to dance at all in the last few years.

But as the music changed to a slower song he sucked in a breath. Slow dancing he could do.

This was private. This was just him and her. No one watching. And he couldn't watch Gabrielle much longer without touching. He moved more purposely, catching Gabrielle's hand while she danced and pulling her against him.

'I think the tempo's changed.'

He could feel the curves of her breasts pressed against his chest. One of his hands lingered at the bare skin at her waist and it felt entirely natural for his fingers to gently stroke her soft skin.

She hadn't spoken yet but as he kept his gaze fixed on hers, her pupils dilated, the blackness obliterating the dark chocolate of her irises. She reached one hand up to his shoulder. It was almost like a traditional dance position. The one a million couples dancing at weddings the world over would adopt.

'You're right,' she said huskily, 'the tempo has changed.' She started to sway along to the music in his arms. It was easy for their bodies to move as one. What's more, it seemed completely natural.

He couldn't help the smile appearing on his face. He'd spent the last few days thinking of how it would feel to be in exactly this position. Her rose scent was winding its way around him. He slid his hand from her waist up the smooth skin on her back. She didn't object. In fact, she responded, tugging at his T-shirt and moving both her hands onto his skin. He caught his breath at the feel of her soft hands. Gabrielle wasn't shy. Both hands slid around to the front. She was smiling as she moved them up over his chest. He lowered his head, pressing his forehead on hers.

'Not long until Paris,' he whispered.

She glanced towards the opening of the tent. 'I don't know if I want to wait until Paris.' The huskiness of her voice made the blood rush around his body.

He walked her backwards against the table, pressing her against it as his lips came into contact with hers. She tasted of chocolate. Of coffee. She responded instantly. Lips opening, matching his every move. His hands moved to her firm breasts, slipping under the wire of her bra and filling his hands.

She arched her back and he caught her unspoken message, moving his other hand to unclip her bra at the back and release her breasts more freely for his attention.

She pushed herself back onto the table, opening her legs and pulling him towards her, a little noise escaping from the back of her throat. She made a grab for his T-shirt, pulling it over his head.

He laid her back onto the table, concentrating his lips on the paler skin at her throat then around her ear. The little sigh she gave made his blood race even faster.

Then he felt her hands on his shoulders. She wasn't pushing him away but her grip was firm. He eased back, connecting with her gaze and rapid breathing. At the base of her throat he could see a little flickering pulse.

'Gabrielle?' he groaned.

Her gaze was steady. 'Four days,' she whispered. 'In four days, we can do this in Paris.' Her head turned towards the tent entrance again, the flaps held back onto the dark night. It really was wide open to the world; any of the other camp members could appear at a moment's notice.

He drew in a deep breath. She was right. He knew she was right. It didn't matter that he'd be much happier if they could both just tear their clothes off now. For a few seconds he'd lost his normal professional demeanour.

They both had. Gabrielle was the lead professional on this mission. He had to remember that.

The spark between them had been building every day. Right now he felt as if the electricity they were generating could light up the Chrysler Building. There was something about this woman that got under his skin. Right from his first sight of her dancing around this very tent. It had been so long since he'd felt a connection like this that he was half-afraid if he closed his eyes for a second it would disappear. He couldn't let that happen. He *wouldn't* let that happen.

Four days. He could put a lid on it for four days. He might even message a friend to ask for a recommendation for a more private Paris hotel than the one he usually bedded down in.

He stepped back. Keeping in contact with Gabrielle Cartier's skin was a definite recipe for self-implosion.

He smiled. 'Four days isn't so long.' He grabbed his T-shirt and pulled it over his head as he walked towards the tent flaps.

He turned as he reached the entrance and started walking backwards. He winked at her. 'Watch out, Paris. Here we come.'

CHAPTER FOUR

THE DEBRIEF HAD been quicker than expected.
Their data collection had been fastidious. It
helped correlate the numbers of cases of pulmo-
nary TB and MDR-TB in Narumba. The data
spreadsheet recording all the side effects of any
of the medications would be analysed by their
pharmacy colleagues, and the extra information
on childhood weight and nutrition would be col-
lated for international statistics. The longest part
of the review was around the safety aspects of the
team that had gone out to replace them.

Sullivan had already made some recommen-
dations. Three of the team members this time
were male and extra interpreters were available.

Six missions had returned at the same time and
right now every member from each of the missions was jammed around the booths in a bar in
Paris. Drinks filled the tables. Laughter filled
the air. After a few months of quiet it didn't take
long for the thumping music and loud voices to
start reverberating around his head.

Gabrielle seemed in her element. The girl knew

how to let her hair down. Literally. Her glossy dark curls tumbled around her shoulders, her brown eyes were shining and the tanned skin on her arms drew more than a few admiring glances. She was dressed comfortably, in well-fitting jeans and a black scoop-neck vest trimmed with black sequins. A thin gold chain decorated her neck, with some kind of locket nestling down between her breasts.

Maybe it was the buzz in the air. Maybe it was just the electricity of Paris. Or maybe it was the novelty of having some down time. But one part of him couldn't fully relax.

He'd drunk a few beers and joined in a few stories but the undercurrent between him and Gabrielle seemed to bubble under the surface. This whole thing seemed like a preface to the main event.

It could be it was simply easier to concentrate on the here and now than the future. The future would mean finally having to think about going back home to Oregon to deal with his father's belongings. His stomach curled at the mere thought. It was pathetic really. He was a thirty-three-year-old guy—and he'd served in some of the toughest areas of the world—but the thought of bundling up some clothes and taking them to goodwill made his blood run cold.

It was so much easier not to acknowledge it

and just move on to the next job. Take the next emergency call that came in from Doctors Without Borders and head off on the next mission.

He excused himself and stood up, walking towards the men's room. The corridor here was little quieter, a little darker. His footsteps slowed and he leaned against the wall, closing his eyes for a second.

He couldn't talk about this. He wouldn't talk about this. He and his dad had been on their own for so long after his mother had been killed in a riding accident when he was three. All he could remember of her was a smell and a swish of warm soft hair. He had plenty of photographs of her but when he closed his eyes, it was the touch and the smell that flooded his senses.

It meant that he and his dad had been a team. For as long as he could remember there had been an unshakable bond. His father had refused to be stationed anywhere without his son. Japan, Italy, UK and Germany had all played a part in his multinational upbringing. There had hardly been any discipline because he'd never been a bad kid. He'd never wanted to disappoint his dad. And the day he'd told him he wanted to do his medical degree and serve, tears had glistened in his father's eyes.

The sudden phone call out of the blue had been like a knife through his heart. His father had never had a day's illness in his life. The post mortem had shown an aortic aneurysm. The surgeon in Sullivan hated that. It was something that was fixable. Something that could have been detected and fixed. His father could have had another twenty years of life.

Instead, Sullivan had been left to unlock the door on the Hood River house and be overwhelmed by the familiar smells. Of wood, of fishing, of cleaning materials and of just…him.

The house that had been full of happy memories seemed to have a permanent black cloud over it now. Anytime he thought of returning his stomach curled in a familiar knot. It was hardly appropriate for a former soldier.

There was a nudge at his side. 'Hey, you, what are you doing, sleeping on the job?'

He almost laughed out loud at the irony. She'd no idea how much the art of sleeping had escaped him in the last few years.

Gabrielle gave a smile and moved in front of him, matching his pose by leaning on the wall and folding her arms across her chest. He couldn't help but smile.

'Was I boring you that much?' she teased.

He reached out and touched her bare shoulder, running his finger down the smooth soft skin on her outer arm. 'Oh, believe me, you weren't boring me at all.'

Her eyes twinkled. 'So, why are you hiding back here?' Her folded arms accentuated her cleavage and she caught his gaze and raised her eyebrows.

He let out a laugh. It was one of the things he liked best about her—a woman who was happy in her own skin. If only every woman could be like that.

'I wasn't hiding.' He grinned. 'I was contemplating a way to get you back here on your own.'

'Hmm…' She moved a little closer. 'And why would you be doing that, Dr Darcy?'

He loved the way his name tripped off her tongue. The accent sent shivers to places that were already wide awake. Her hand reached up and drummed a little beat on his shoulder.

His hand moved forward, catching her around the waist and pulling her up against him, letting her know in no uncertain terms what his intentions were.

Her eyes widened and her hands fastened around his neck. 'I'm assuming you made good on our plans.'

'You could say that.'

'What does that mean? Where are we staying?'

In the dim light of the corridor her brown eyes seemed even darker. Full of promise. Full of mystery. The feel of her warm curves pressing against him spoke of another promise.

He wound his fingers through her hair. 'I might have booked us in somewhere a little bit special.'

Her eyebrows raised again. 'You have?'

'I have. It seems a shame to waste any more time.'

She rose up on tiptoe and whispered in his ear, 'And is that what we're doing, Dr Darcy, wasting time?'

Her warm breath danced against the skin behind his ear. He let his eyes close for a second again before he groaned out loud and made a grab for her hand.

'Let's go.'

She didn't resist in the slightest. 'Let me grab my jacket,' she shouted as she let go of his hand and weaved her way through the crowd. He gave a quick nod and headed over to the bar, pulling out his wallet and settling the current bar tab. He didn't want to wait for the flying euros as they fought over who wanted to contribute. To some the bar tab might have seemed large. To people who'd been in other countries for three months, it didn't even come to the equivalent of a night out every weekend.

He waited at the door as Gabrielle gave a few people a hug and planted kisses on some cheeks. As she leaned over the table he had a prime view of those well-fitting jeans. Boy, did they hug her curves—but right now the only place he wanted to see those jeans was on the floor of their suite in the Mandarin Oriental.

She didn't walk towards him. She bounced. It was almost a skip. He couldn't wipe the smile off his face as her gaze connected with his and she made her way back over to join him.

'Ready, soldier?' she said as he held the door open.

He was too busy watching her moves, too busy focusing on those long legs and curves, too busy watching her eyes to notice anything else.

It all happened so quickly.

Gabrielle took a few steps out of his reach. She was teasing him, taunting him, spinning around to face him, pulling down her jacket to reveal one shoulder.

One second he could see her delicious smile, the next second his vision was entirely obscured.

It happened in the blink of an eye.

Six men—all dressed in black—surrounded her.

It seemed as though time stopped. At least it did for Sullivan. He'd never really suffered from flashbacks of his time in the army, but now adrenaline pumped through him.

He might be a medic, but he'd always made sure he could give the guys from Special Forces a run for their money.

Tunnel vision. That's what some people called

it. But for Sullivan it was different. It was ultimate focus.

He moved quickly. The first guy he just grabbed between the shoulder blades and flung backwards to the floor. The guys on either side took a couple of punches to the face. The guy at ten o'clock got a swift kick to the chest, the guy at two o'clock a karate-style chop.

But the man directly behind Gabrielle had more time—if mere seconds—to react. He grabbed Gabrielle and spun around, shielding her body with his own.

Noise had faded as he'd moved. He hadn't thought. He'd just reacted. It took another second to realise Gabrielle was screaming. The kick from behind took the legs from him, but the punch to the head hardly registered.

'Stop it! Stop it!' Gabrielle screamed, extricating herself from under the dark-suited man's grip.

An arm clamped around Sullivan's neck and he reached up to grab it, ducking forward and throwing the man over his shoulder without a thought. The second punch to the side of his head annoyed him.

Who were these men and why were they attacking them?

Or were they?

He gave his head a shake. Only about five seconds had passed.

He pressed his hand to the ground, getting ready to jump back to his feet, when Gabrielle moved into the middle of the sprawled bodies. '*Stop!*' she shouted, standing with her legs spread apart and her arms held wide.

All heads turned in her direction. She turned to the man behind her and pointed at Sullivan. 'He,' she spat out furiously, 'is with me!' She pointed her finger to her chest to emphasise her words.

Her angry gaze connected with Sullivan. 'And they...' she looked around at the dark-suited men, and let out a huge sigh '...I guess are with me too.'

'What?' Sullivan shook his head. Maybe that last knock to the head had been harder than he'd thought. What on earth was she talking about?

He stood up and looked around. A few of the guys were shooting him looks of disgust and dusting off their suits.

He could sense one of them standing directly behind him. The guy was practically growling.

Sullivan stepped forward. His first instinct was still to protect Gabrielle. 'Are you okay? What on earth is going on?'

He slid his hand to the side of her waist. She was trembling. Her whole body was trembling. But he could see the determined jut to her chin. She pressed her lips tight together as she tried to compose herself.

She spun around, facing the guy who'd shielded her body with his. 'Arun, what is going on? Why are you here?'

The dark-skinned man gave a little bow. 'Your Majesty. Your brother—the former Prince Andreas—has abdicated. He left the country a few hours ago. We have to take you back to get you sworn in as Head of State.'

'Your...what?'

Sullivan gave his head a second shake and glanced downwards for a second. Was he secretly out cold or hallucinating? The dark-skinned man had a strange accent, Middle Eastern mixed with a distinctly British edge.

Gabrielle swayed. Two sets of hands reached out automatically to catch her. Arun's and his own.

'He's what? Andreas has done *what*?' Her voice rose in pitch and she started pacing in circles. 'Where is he? Where has he gone? Why hasn't he spoken to me? He can't do this.' She flung her hands in the air. 'He can't just walk away from Mirinez! Who does that? Who walks away from their country?'

Five sets of eyes blinked and averted their gaze for a second. Sullivan felt something washing over him. Unease.

Arun kept his gaze solidly on Gabrielle and his voice low and steady. 'Princess Gabrielle, it's time to return home. It's time to come back to Mirinez. Your country needs you.'

Panic flooded Gabrielle's face. She pulled her phone from her bag and started pressing buttons furiously. 'Andreas. I need to speak to Andreas. He emailed me a few weeks ago. I told him I'd get in touch when I got back.'

Arun pulled an envelope from his pocket as he glanced at his watch. 'He's currently on a flight to New York. He left you this.'

Her hand was shaking as she reached for the envelope. She pulled the letter out and took a few steps away, head bowed as she read.

Sullivan looked around and put his hands on his hips. 'It's one of these things, isn't it?' He took a few paces, glancing towards every corner on the street. 'You're filming us somewhere and it's all a set-up—it's all a big joke.'

Arun met his gaze and shook his head, giving a few rapid instructions to the other men, who changed positions.

Gabrielle was still reading the letter. Her body was rigid, her face pale. She crumpled the letter between her hands.

Several of their colleagues came out from the bar. 'Gabrielle? Sullivan? Is everything okay?'

The shout seemed to jolt Gabrielle into action. She pushed her hair back from her face. She gave a wave. 'Hi, Connor, Matt, everything's fine. Just a little misunderstanding.'

Connor frowned and shot Sullivan a wary glance before giving a brief nod and disappearing back inside the bar.

'A misunderstanding?' Sullivan walked up to Gabrielle. 'We walk out of a bar and get attacked by six goons and you think that's a misunderstanding?'

She glanced sideways. 'Shh,' she said quickly. She stared down at the crumpled paper in her hand.

Sullivan took a deep breath. 'Are you going to let me into the secret here? What's with the princess stuff—and why are these guys attacking us?'

Gabrielle gave a huge sigh, her shoulders slumping. She shook her head. 'They're not attacking us. At least, not me. They're my protection detail.'

'Since when do you have protection detail? Where were these guys when we were in Narumba?' He shook his head. 'And princess? Mirinez? Is this all some kind of joke?'

Tears glistened in Gabrielle's eyes. 'Believe me, Sullivan. I wish it was.' Her gaze was drawn back to the six men. 'I have a protection detail now because I've just inherited the title of Head of State of Mirinez. It's a small principality—you've probably never heard of it.'

Sullivan narrowed his gaze and racked his brain. He'd lived in enough places to know most of the geography of the world. 'I have heard of it. It's in the Med. A few hours from here, in fact.' He tried to pull what he could remember from the vestiges of his mind. 'It's a tax haven, isn't it?'

Gabrielle made a kind of exasperated sound. 'Yes, yes, it is. My brother inherited the title. He was Head of State.' She held up the crumpled paper. 'But it seems he's had a change of heart.'

Sullivan felt as if he were waiting for someone to pinch him. Or punch him—but, no, two guys had already done that.

'You're a princess?'

She nodded.

'We spent two weeks together in Narumba. We were just about to head off to a hotel suite and do…whatever. And you're a princess. And you didn't tell me.' It was almost as if saying it out loud actually clarified it in his head.

For a second she looked pained. But that passed fleetingly, quickly replaced by a stubborn look. 'It wasn't important. I'm a doctor. That's what you needed to know in Narumba. And even though I was a princess it wasn't important. I didn't need to fulfil that role any more. When I work for Doctors Without Borders I'm just Gabrielle.'

In a way he could understand that. He could. But it still annoyed him. Would he have looked at

Gabrielle any differently if he'd known she was a princess? He didn't think so. But it was just the fact she hadn't told him that irked.

He kept his voice steady. 'You didn't need to fulfil that role…but now you do.' He met her gaze. 'So what now?'

There it was again. That little flash of something. It wasn't horror. It wasn't fear. It was just… something. That thing that you saw in a kid's eyes when his parent made him do something he really didn't want to do. It looked almost like regret about having to be there. Having to take part in that point of life.

Gabrielle looked down. 'I guess… I guess…' She lifted her gaze. 'I guess I have to go back. I have a duty.'

Her voice shook and her eyes reflected all the things she wasn't saying out loud. The upset. The shock.

He reached up and touched her cheek, 'If you don't want to go back, you shouldn't have to go. You're a free woman, Gabrielle.'

She blinked and he could see the tears hovering in the corners of her eyes. She pressed her hand up to her chest. 'But I'm not. Not now. I haven't been back to Mirinez for the last few years.' She gave a sad smile. 'Being a doctor gave me the life I wanted. I never wanted to rule. I never wanted to be Head of State. That was always Andreas's job.'

'But he's bailed.'

His blunt words brought a hint of a wry smile to her lips. 'He's bailed.'

She sucked in a deep breath and looked over at her protection detail. It was almost as if something had just flashed into her brain.

He had the oddest feeling—like a million little men with muddy feet were stamping all over the next few hours of his life.

'What does this mean for you?'

All the warmth and fun that had been in Gabrielle's face earlier had vanished. She had that strange pallor about her—the kind that a patient had before they fainted.

He put his hand on her shoulder. Visions of the night he'd planned had just slipped down the nearest drain. The fancy hotel suite and room service he'd looked forward to sharing with Gabrielle would remain a figment of his very vivid imagination.

He could go back to the bar and get drunk with the others.

He could sign up for another mission, avoid taking that flight home—yet again.

Gabrielle squeezed her eyes closed for a second.

The words were out before he thought about

them. 'Gabrielle, if you need to go home, if you're worried, I'll come with you.'

She opened her eyes. They widened slightly. It was almost as if she couldn't think straight.

She shook her head. 'Don't. Don't do that. Don't come with me. I can't ask you to do that. It's not fair.'

'What's not fair?'

She threw up her hands. 'This. All of it.' She glanced over her shoulder and lowered her voice. 'I *don't* want to go back. I can't ask you to come with me.'

He shrugged his shoulders. 'You haven't asked. I've offered.'

She paused. He could see the hesitation in her face. But she shook her head again. 'No, it just won't work.'

He hated the expression she currently had on her face. She was saying no, but his gut instincts could tell she didn't mean it. And Sullivan had always prided himself on his instincts. It was the one part of him that thankfully hadn't dulled in the last few years.

He held up his hands. 'Well, okay, then. I don't even know where Mirinez is. But I'm sure I can find it on a map. I can still get there, you know— with or without you.'

She gulped. That edge of panic was still in her

eyes and they were shining with unshed tears. He could sense the emotion in her.

He didn't need to go to home. He'd put it off for three years. He could put it off a whole lot longer. It didn't matter that he'd almost persuaded himself that this time he finally would go. It wasn't like he really wanted to.

Part of him ached. And he couldn't quite work out if it was entirely for the woman in front of him, or for the recognition that once again he was avoiding the one thing that he shouldn't.

The thought kick-started him.

'I'm coming with you, Gabrielle. You don't need to say a single word. I know you're shocked. I know this wasn't in your plans.' He raised his eyebrows and put his arm around her shoulders. 'We'll talk about the fact you didn't tell me you were a princess later.' He was half-joking. He wanted to try and take the edge off her nerves and worry.

She sucked in a breath. He could tell her brain was churning, thinking of a whole lot of other reasons to say no.

He leaned forward and whispered in her ear, 'You need a friend right now. That's me.'

Gabrielle was a princess. This was the woman he'd flirted with like mad for the last two weeks, had worked alongside and he'd dreamed of exploring beneath the confines of those clothes.

Were you actually supposed to do that with a *princess*?

Part of him wondered if there was some ancient law against those kind of thoughts—let alone any actions.

She tilted her chin up to his ear. Her voice was trembling. 'Thank you.'

Every emotion was written on her face. She was scared. She was worried. She was overwhelmed.

This was a whole new Gabrielle. The one he'd worked with over the last two weeks had been confident, efficient and extremely competent at her job—even when under pressure and difficult circumstances. She had a cool head in a crisis.

This Gabrielle looked as if she could burst into tears.

Just how bad could Mirinez be?

He glanced over at the security detail, some still glowering at him as they talked in low voices. These were the people in charge of protecting Gabrielle? He wasn't entirely impressed. The only one that actually gave him any confidence was Arun.

He gave a squeeze of her shoulders. What on earth had he just got himself into? 'I guess it's time to visit Mirinez.'

CHAPTER FIVE

FOUR HOURS LATER their plane left Charles De Gaulle airport. Their departure had been a whirlwind.

One of the security detail had sidled up to him with a suspicious glare and muttered to him in French, 'Special Forces?'

'Surgeon, US Army. I've done two tours of Helmand Province and spent the last three years with Doctors Without Borders.'

The man blinked at the quick response in his own language. He sauntered off again.

Sullivan was pretty sure that his details were now being fed through every security system that they had. He didn't care. There was nothing for them to find.

The private plane was sumptuous. There were wide cream leather seats, a table in front of them with an attendant waiting on their every need.

The protection detail was on the same plane, but Gabrielle spent most of her time on the phone to someone in Mirinez, answering emails or staring out of the window forlornly.

As the plane descended for landing Sullivan

leaned over and looked out. The vast picturesque landscape took him by surprise. Mountains, green fields, river and trees. As they skirted the edges of the coastline there was a huge array of harbours filled with bobbing boats and a number of cruise ships anchored in the ports. It seemed Mirinez was quite a tourist destination.

The plane banked to the left and they passed over a city, which was overlooked by a cream castle halfway up the mountain.

'This is Mirinez?' he asked. From her reactions he'd thought they'd be landing somewhere stuck in the virtual dark ages. From a few thousand feet up Mirinez looked like a playground for the rich and famous.

She nodded as she drummed her fingers nervously on the table. 'Yes.'

His voice seemed to focus her. She pointed out of the window. 'This is our main harbour. Chabonnex is our capital city. It's the most popular tourist destination.'

He looked up towards the mountain. 'And the royal family stays in the castle?'

She gave a wry smile. 'Yes. That's one thing that's never changed in the history of Mirinez.'

Sullivan spoke carefully. 'So, there's just you and Andreas left?'

Gabrielle nodded. 'Our father died a few years ago after a massive stroke.' She sighed. 'He wouldn't listen. He liked the good life. He was overweight, had high blood pressure and cholesterol and wouldn't listen to a word I said to him.' Her voice softened. 'I think, in truth, he just missed my mother.'

He felt a pang. 'What happened to your mother?'

It took a few seconds for her to answer. 'She had heart surgery. We thought it would be routine. She'd had a valve replaced due to rheumatic heart disease as a child. There had always been a question about whether my mother should have children.' Gabrielle gave a little smile. 'But apparently she'd been very determined. The heart valve needed to be replaced and she went in for surgery…'

Her voice tailed off and Sullivan didn't need to ask any more. Cardiac surgery might not be his speciality but any surgery carried risks.

He wanted to reach over and squeeze her hand but the truth was he wasn't quite sure what his role here was. He still wasn't certain why he'd insisted on coming. A tiny part of him recognised that being here was easier than going home. Was coming here really just an excuse to avoid that?

He still hadn't really gauged the strong attraction between them. Getting up close and personal with a colleague on a mission, or back home, was entirely different from travelling to a country with a princess about to be made Head of State. If Gabrielle could barely get her head around this, how could he?

She turned towards him. Her smile was nervous, but the gleam in her eye was still there.

She lifted her hand as if she were about to touch his cheek. But her hand froze in mid-air and she glanced behind them towards her security detail. Their gazes connected almost as if the touch had still happened. The buzz that he'd first felt in Narumba was still clearly there.

They'd just never quite reached the place that they'd been heading to.

She pulled her hand back, her dark eyes intense. 'Thank you,' she whispered. 'Thank you for coming with me.'

The reply was easy. 'Any time.' He leaned back as they settled back in their seats for landing.

Mirinez. Another country to check off his list on the map he'd had since he was a child. He had no idea what would come next.

Her stomach couldn't settle. All the way up the mountain in the limousine her eyes were fixed on the castle.

Sullivan seemed relaxed. He wasn't demanding her attention, just offering the occasional smile of support. She was secretly glad he'd insisted on coming but she was also confused. The intensity of Paris and Narumba and all the things she'd intended to do with Sullivan seemed so far out of her grasp. Starting something now would be unfair. She hadn't even had a chance to contemplate what her role would be in Mirinez. They'd only ever spoken of ten days together. A fling. She couldn't weigh him down with the royal duties that were about to descend on her.

All she knew was that he felt like the one solid thing around her. And that didn't refer to his muscular stance—though that wasn't exactly a problem either.

Arun had been furious that the royal security detail of six had been beaten by one unknown quantity. Gabrielle didn't know whether to laugh or cry.

She was furious with Andreas. *Furious.* She'd never known anger like it.

Her entire life it had been made clear that Prince Andreas would inherit the title and rule the principality. It had never even occurred to her that might not happen. Their father's death had been a shock to them both, but it had only moved the inevitability of Andreas's role a little closer.

She'd spent the last few hours in the plane rethinking every conversation, every contact, every text, every email that they'd ever shared.

And she was still furious. It seemed that life in

Mirinez wasn't Hollywood enough for Andreas's wife. She'd made him choose. And he had.

The last few years out of the spotlight had been blissful for Gabrielle. She liked living under the radar. She liked being a doctor, thinking like a doctor, acting like a doctor. That was the life she had chosen.

As the limousine turned and drove between the stone-carved pillars and through the wrought-iron gates Gabrielle sucked in her breath. She'd loved living here as a child. It was only as an adult she'd felt cloistered by the views and opinions around her.

The limousine door opened and she stepped out. The stones crunched beneath her feet as the cold-tipped air from the mountain swept around her. The cream-coloured palace loomed above her, built on the side of the mountain, looking over the city of Chabonnex below.

The city was stunning. From here it looked like a village built for tiny people, filled with tram lines and townhouses. There were no skyscrapers or tower blocks in Mirinez.

She walked up the steps to the palace entrance. The doors were wide open and the familiar scent of pine, lemon and old oak filled the air. The palace had always smelled like this. She walked across the black and white marble floor. She'd been told that the palace in Mirinez had been based on designs of Blenheim Palace in the UK. Mirinez's was like a miniature version. Every room had high ceilings with ornate plaster designs, lavish chandeliers and wood-panelled walls.

Her father's advisor, Franz Hindermann, was waiting. He gave her the briefest of nods. 'Princess Gabrielle, we have much to discuss.'

She nodded in acknowledgement. 'Franz, I've brought a guest with me. A colleague from Doctors Without Borders, Dr Darcy. Will you show him to my apartments?'

Franz couldn't hide the blanching of his face. She was surprised. She'd long since been an adult—what did he expect?

'Ab-bout your apartments,' he stammered as he handed over a clipboard filled with sheets of paper.

'Yes?'

'Well… I've moved you.'

'What?'

So that's what the hesitation had been for. 'Why have you moved me?'

Franz cleared his throat. 'Prince Andreas moved out rather quickly. And he took all of his belongings with him. His last instructions were to move you into the royal apartments.'

A chill spread through her. So this was real. This was actually happening. The apartments that had housed her mother and father, and then her brother and his wife, were now hers.

She'd spent years with a view that looked out over the mountain and stables. A view she'd loved.

Now it would consist of something else entirely. 'Oh, okay,' she said quickly. 'Put Dr Darcy in the rooms next to mine.'

Franz nodded and hurried away.

Sullivan appeared at her shoulder, holding his bag. 'You okay?'

She turned towards him. Right now she wanted to turn back the clock twelve hours. She wanted to go back to the bar in Paris where there was wine and laughing and a really hot guy in the corridor. She wanted to close her eyes, take his hand and let him lead her to the promised hotel suite where she could peel off the clothes that had kept them apart for the last two weeks.

She didn't want to think about being a princess. Her country. A brother who had abdicated and disappeared. She didn't want to think about the responsibility. She couldn't even begin to imagine how this would affect the life she wanted to live.

She rested her palm against his chest, feeling his defined muscles and warm skin through the thin cotton of his T-shirt. Somehow being around this man grounded her. Focused her.

It let her think about the things she really

wanted to do. Patients. Medicines. The next mission. Dark nights. Tangled sheets and so, so much more.

'No, I'm not,' she said clearly. 'But I will be.'

Sullivan's eyebrows rose for a second and his familiar grin spread across his face. 'Let me know what you need.'

He leaned forward and whispered in her ear, 'In every sense.'

The tight feeling in her belly unwound, spreading warmth that blossomed outwards. She pulled back, staring at her hand. She shouldn't have touched him. It was confusing things. For her and for him. She couldn't meet his enquiring gaze. She just gave the briefest of nods towards Franz and watched Sullivan follow him up the main staircase.

After twenty-four hours Sullivan felt as if he was having an out-of-body experience. People didn't move around this palace—they glided. The volume control seemed to be in a permanently muted state. He wondered what would happen if he went back to the main entrance, stood with arms and legs apart and let out some kind of jungle scream—or maybe even, in keeping with Europe, a kind of yodel.

He wasn't used to being around so much quietness. Quietness reminded him of a few occasions he'd been out retrieving wounded casualties in Helmand Provence and he'd had the signal from the one of other soldiers to keep absolutely quiet. Those days were long past and he had no real desire to go back there.

Or to the silence of his father's house.

Plus, he was bored. The wonder of living in a palace was for five-year-old girls in pink fluffy dresses. Not for guys used to living out of a backpack for three months at a time in places where running water wasn't always available.

He wasn't working. And if he wasn't working he had time to think.

Time he neither needed nor wanted. Thinking might take him down a road he didn't want to travel.

Someone had bought him a suit. Last time he'd worn a suit had been at a job interview long ago. There hadn't been much call for one since.

He'd picked it up, held it against himself and laughed. It was designed to fit a man of much smaller proportions. He doubted he could even fit a thigh into those trousers.

There was always a member of palace staff floating around outside the rooms. 'Why do I have a suit?' he'd asked a small nervous-looking individual.

'Mr Hindermann th-thought you might n-need

one,' he stammered, 'if you were accompanying the princess to any official events.'

Sullivan raised his eyebrows. The thought hadn't even entered his mind. He wasn't here to do anything like that. That would make him— what—some kind of man candy? He shuddered as wicked thoughts crossed his mind.

'Get me a kilt.'

'Wha-at?' The man looked even more nervous.

'A kilt. I don't wear suits. I have Scottish heritage. I'll only wear a kilt.'

He was doing his best not to laugh. He had no more Scottish ancestry than an American apple pie, but it would teach them to ask and not to *presume*.

'Do you know where Arun is?'

Redness was creeping up the smaller man's face. 'Mr Aliman will be in the security headquarters.'

'And that is?' Sullivan pointed down the corridor and took a few steps in that direction.

The man pointed. 'Down the stairs, into the west wing, take a left, another left, a right, a left and up the second flight of stairs.'

Sullivan blinked. Then smiled. 'No problem.'

The palace was bigger than he'd thought. Wings must have added on in later parts of the construction. But the directions were good. Ten minutes later he found Arun.

The dark-skinned man stood as soon as Sullivan appeared at the door. 'Dr Darcy, what can I do for you?'

Sullivan paused for a second, wondering how to approach this. Arun was the only guy in this place that he might actually relate to. He sat down in the chair opposite. 'I was wondering—' he began.

'What to do?' cut in Arun.

Sullivan smiled. He liked a man who got to the point.

'I can arrange a tour for you around Mirinez's capital and historic sites.'

Sullivan couldn't help but roll his eyes. 'Thank you, but no. That's not what I had in mind.'

His eyes caught sight of a thick itinerary with Gabrielle's name on it. He leaned forward, catching the paper at the edge and letting the pages fan past his thumb. '*This* is everything Gabrielle has to do?'

Arun glanced at the empty doorway. 'Princess Gabrielle has been gone for a number of years. There is a lot to catch up on.'

Sullivan folded his arms. 'Why do I feel as if you chose those words very carefully?'

The edges of Arun's lips turned upwards. 'Because you'd be correct. A number of issues have been…'

'Ignored? Pushed under the carpet? Destroyed?'

Arun gave a brief nod. 'It's fair to say that for the last few years Prince Andreas was…distracted. A number of trade agreements with our neighbouring countries urgently need reviewing. Some business deals on behalf of the government, some laws, some peace treaties all need the royal seal of approval.'

Sullivan shook his head. 'What on earth has been going on here?'

Arun shrugged his shoulders and lifted his hands. Sullivan got the distinct impression he secretly wanted to answer, *Not much*.

Sullivan leaned forward and put his elbows on the desk. 'What can I do?' He gestured towards the itinerary. 'It looks like Gabrielle won't have time to breathe, let alone anything else.' He met Arun's gaze and put his cards on the table. 'I don't take kindly to sitting around. Is there a hospital? A clinic I could visit? Somewhere I could make myself useful?'

Arun paused for a second then gave a careful nod. 'You understand healthcare in Mirinez is different from the US?'

Sullivan frowned. 'What does that mean?'

Arun held up his hands again. 'Mirinez is a tax haven. We have many, highly exclusive, state-of-the-art, private hospitals.'

Sullivan leaned back in his chair. 'Is this a tax haven or a plastic surgery haven?'

'Don't the two go hand in hand?' There was a wry expression on Arun's face.

Sullivan didn't even try to stop the exasperated sound coming from his throat. 'What about the citizens of Mirinez? They can't all be millionaires. Where do they go?'

Arun nodded. 'We have a few state hospitals and a few state-funded clinics. We also have a number of semi-private clinics part funded by businesses operating in Mirinez.'

Sullivan stood up. 'That's fine. Take me to some of those.' Then he realised how those words sounded and he lifted his hand in deference. 'Sorry, I'd be grateful if you could find someone to take me somewhere I might actually be useful. I'm a surgeon. My qualifications are available for anyone who needs them.'

Arun was smiling. 'Which one of my men that you punched would you prefer to take you?'

Sullivan winced. 'Yeah, about that…'

Arun nodded. 'You're right. We've rarely had any incidents. Their training needs to be reviewed and updated.'

Sullivan put his hand on his chest. He was trying not to smile at Arun's response. 'But I never said that.'

'You didn't need to.' Arun picked up the phone. 'I'll get someone to meet you at the rear entrance to the west wing—near the stables.'

'The tradesmen's entrance?' he joked.

'Exactly.' Sullivan was starting to really like this guy. His British sense of humour was shining through. 'Where did you go to school?' he asked.

'Gordonstoun.'

'That explains it, then,' he quipped.

'Oh, Dr Darcy?' Arun had a mischievous look on his face. 'Did the suit fit?'

'Not in this lifetime.'

Sullivan headed out the door as the very British laugh followed him down the corridor.

CHAPTER SIX

MIRINEZ FELT LIKE a whirlwind. From the second she'd set foot in the palace Gabrielle hadn't even had time to think.

She'd now sent Andreas seventeen emails and left six voicemails, each one more irate than the last. It wasn't the fact he'd abdicated. Well, it was. But it was also the fact he hadn't been doing the job he should have been doing for the last three years.

She looked at the carved wooden desk that had been in the palace for hundreds of years. Franz had allocated her tasks into piles. And it wasn't simple piles like urgent, important and information.

No, these piles were overdue by two years, overdue by one year. Must be signed today. Must be contacted today.

Then there were sub-piles about legal matters, countries, trade agreements and finance.

She held up her hands. 'What on earth has Andreas been doing? How have things got so bad?'

It shouldn't be like this. It definitely shouldn't. Mirinez was a small principality with a population of forty-five thousand. Her father had managed things comfortably. He'd looked after orders of state, their government, entertained visiting dignitaries, all while keeping up a whole variety of personal interests. Since she was a child, Gabrielle had known the role didn't need to be a full-time job. She'd thought that once Andreas had married his TV star wife, he would have plenty of time to keep her happy. It seemed he'd spent *all* his time keeping her happy and none at all dealing with matters of state.

Right now, if he'd been in the same room she would have wrung his neck with her bare hands.

Franz couldn't even meet her gaze. She reached over and squeezed his hand. 'I'm sorry. I'm just shocked that things have been so neglected. I had no idea Andreas wasn't fulfilling his duties. Why didn't you tell me?'

Franz met her gaze with his slate-grey eyes. 'I was forbidden.'

The words cut through her heart like ice. 'What?'

Franz was a traditionalist. He must be nearly seventy now and had been in the employment of the Mirinez royal family for Gabrielle's entire life. If Andreas had forbidden him to contact her, he would have respected the Prince's wishes. She didn't even want to think what the stress had done to Franz's health.

She was beyond angry. She was furious. Her stomach gave a little flip at the thought of what she'd brought Sullivan into.

She hadn't been upfront about being a princess. But when he'd sensed her momentary panic at returning home he'd insisted on coming back with her. Truth was, whether he liked it or not, Sullivan Darcy was a gentleman.

But the amount of work in front of her was going to consume her every waking minute. She hadn't expected this. He was her guest.

She leaned her head down on the desk as the old-fashioned phone in front of her started to ring. Franz answered it in his usual low voice but his quick change in tone made her sit up again.

'What is it?'

His face was instantly pale. 'There's been an accident in one of the diamond mines. An explosion.'

Gabrielle was on her feet in a second. 'How many?'

Franz was confused. 'How many what?'

She grabbed her jacket. 'How many casualties and what mine?'

Franz spoke again then stammered his reply, 'Around f-forty, mostly b-burns. It's the Pieper mine.'

She headed for the door as thoughts flooded through her head. Burns. Sullivan was a surgeon. After working in Helmand Province he was bound to have experience with explosive injuries and burns.

She spun around. 'Someone find Sullivan. Tell him I'll need his assistance.'

Franz put down the phone. 'Princess Gabrielle?'

She was already walking back out the door but something about his anxious tone stopped her. 'What?'

'Dr Darcy. He's already there.'

'He's *what*?'

Franz gulped. 'He's helping co-ordinate the rescue effort.'

She didn't wait for a driver. She got into the nearest palace car and just floored it. At least she tried to. Arun stepped out dead centre in front of the car as she reached the palace gates.

'Move!' she screamed.

He calmly walked around to the driver's side. 'Move over,' he replied smoothly.

She blinked, then took a deep breath and moved over. He slid into the driver's seat and drove down the mountain as if an avalanche was chasing them. But Arun had the skill and expertise to handle the car at speed.

He pressed a button on the steering wheel, connected to his control room, and spoke in rapid

French. A few seconds later, another voice came on the line. It took Gabrielle a few seconds to realise who it was. By the time she did, Arun had disconnected.

They reached the bottom of the mountain and, instead of turning right, towards the diamond mine, he turned left.

'Where are we going?' shouted Gabrielle. 'People need help.' She could hear the sound of sirens in the distance. 'Was that Sullivan on the phone?' Her brain was still trying to fathom how fluent his French had been.

Arun made the next corner on practically two wheels. 'We're not going to the mine. We're going to St George's.'

'St George's?' She was confused. It was one of the most prestigious hospitals in Mirinez—mainly for private patients. From what she could remember, it did have a fully functioning small emergency department that treated private patients.

'Why are we going there?'

Arun glanced at her as they turned down the main road towards the hospital. 'Because apparently Sullivan has taken over.'

CHAPTER SEVEN

SPEAKING NUMEROUS LANGUAGES in Mirinez was definitely a bonus. So far he'd used French, Italian, German, English and a smattering of Chinese.

He didn't normally contemplate the big picture—but fate had certainly played a part in his being there.

His reluctant security host Mikel had shown him St George's Hospital and introduced him to the director only an hour earlier. The director had made a few casual enquiries about Sullivan's availability as a surgeon and his areas of expertise. What he hadn't expected was for Sullivan to turn up two hours later with a number of casualties from the mine blast.

Mikel, who had spent most of the morning growling at Sullivan and giving one-syllable answers to his questions, had been surprisingly smart when they'd first heard the explosion.

The ground had shaken underneath them as they'd stood in the car park.

Sullivan had moved right into combat mode. 'What's that? Where did that come from?'

Mikel had looked around for a few seconds. 'It must be the mine.'

Sullivan had sped back into the hospital and shouted to the director, 'I need a bag for emergency supplies. We think something's happened at the mine.'

He hadn't waited. He'd moved through the department he'd just been shown around and started grabbing gloves, wound pads, saline and everything else he could lay his hands on. The director had hesitated for a second, then shouted to another member of staff as he'd watched the pile on the trolley grow. Sullivan glanced over his shoulder. 'Do you have ambulances you can send? And give me a couple of members of staff too.'

It wasn't a request. It was an order. Military mode had washed back over him like an old familiar blanket, and thankfully no one had argued. A few minutes later he'd had a bag of supplies and a nurse in the back of the car as Mikel sped towards the mine.

The main gates were wide open. Smoke was spiralling into the sky. People were running everywhere. There was a huge cloud of choking dust hanging in the air.

It only took a few seconds for Sullivan to surmise who was supposed to be in charge. He ran over to a man in a bright yellow fluorescent jacket. 'Sullivan Darcy, doctor. Where do you need me?' He repeated it in French and Italian and the man replied quickly.

'Over there,' he said, pointing to a large grey cabin. 'That's where the casualties are coming up.'

'Who is bringing them up?'

'The other miners.'

'Are there still casualties below ground?'

He nodded. Sullivan thought quickly. 'Ambulances are on their way. I'll triage those in the cabin. Get a report from the mine. If they need medical assistance down there, I can go.'

He moved quickly. The cabin was obviously used for occasional first aid and minor injuries but the first-aid kit must have been used up within seconds of seeing the first casualties. He kept the nurse next to him. She was used to working in a calm hospital environment and he'd obviously taken her well out of her comfort zone. But to her credit she was cool and efficient.

There were a huge variety of injuries—penetrating wounds, head and eye injuries, breathing difficulties, a few obvious broken bones. But the majority of injuries were burns—something he specialised in. It didn't help that every single patient was covered in a layer of smudged dust.

He threw some bags of saline at the nurse. 'We need to try and keep things clean. Irrigate everything that's burned. Remove any clothing or jewellery if you can do it without causing any damage. See if the kitchen has cling wrap. If they do, just put a clean layer across any burn. And keep the burn victims warm—ask for blankets. We don't want them becoming hypothermic. If anyone has a penetrating injury, look at it and patch it. If anyone's bleeding profusely, give me a shout. Triage One, Two and Three. One for the people who need to go to hospital first. Two for those who also need to go but aren't in immediate danger. Three for those who can wait for a limited period.'

She nodded and got to work. Mikel appeared at his side. 'What do you want me to do?'

Sullivan paused only for a second. 'I'm either going to ask you to transport some patients who are stable, or to come down the mine with me. What's your preference?'

Mikel gave a quick nod. 'Wherever you need me.'

Sullivan smiled. He hadn't given Mikel enough credit. He suspected he was a former soldier too—he was obviously a team player. He hadn't panicked when the explosion had happened, and he was happy to take direction and go where he was needed. This man wasn't scared.

Ten minutes later, when he and Mikel descended into the mine, along with one of the engineers, he was glad of the company. Four men were trapped by falling rocks and equipment. No one had known if it was safe to move them to pull them out from where they were trapped and Sullivan and the engineer did a quick assessment of each casualty. Two were able to be slid out slowly once the debris above them had been removed or propped up.

Another was more complicated. He had a serious penetrating wound and burns. By that time, more emergency services had arrived and Sullivan must have used seven bags of saline to saturate wounds, as well as putting in lines to increase fluids and administer some pain relief.

Half an hour later the ambulance he was in pulled up outside St George's. Gabrielle was standing, waiting, in the ambulance bay wearing an apron and gloves. She pulled back as she saw him. 'Where have you been?'

He looked down. Every part of his clothes was covered in dust. He reached up and wiped his forehead, leaving his hand covered in a sooty black mess. He shrugged. 'Down the mine.'

She shook her head and moved into professional mode. 'What have you got?'

He jumped out and pulled the gurney. 'Rufus Bahn, miner. Serious penetrating chest injury.'

She pointed straight ahead. 'The resus room is waiting—once you've washed.'

He nodded and walked quickly. Gabrielle's hair was pulled up in a ponytail on the top of her head. She had on a dress and a pair of strange clogs. She caught him staring and shrugged. 'I didn't have time to change. One of the nurses loaned me her spare shoes.'

Two nurses were waiting in the resus room. Both looked frazzled. Gabrielle gave him a smile as she acknowledged what he'd seen. 'St George's has never dealt with a major accident before. We had to call in some staff from a few surrounding hospitals.'

'Any with trauma experience?'

She shook her head as she put a probe on Mr Bahn's finger, checked his airway and slipped an oxygen mask over his face. As Sullivan tried to wash the worst of the soot and dust off, she scanned Mr Bahn's body, found the cannula she was obviously looking for and drew up some drugs. 'What's he had?'

He pulled on a paper gown and some gloves. 'Just a litre of IV saline.'

'I'm going to give him some morphine for the pain and some steroids for the swelling around his chest area.'

He nodded in agreement. He wasn't quite sure of the last time Gabrielle had dealt with an emergency situation. Any medic working for Doctors

Without Borders could experience just about any situation.

Gabrielle seemed calm and confident, that was good enough for him. She'd tell him if she was feeling out of her depth.

She looked at the penetrating chest wound as he motioned to the radiographer. The mobile X-ray machine was wheeled in and Gabrielle glanced over at him.

He pointed to the door. 'You go out, I'll monitor his airway. I don't want to leave him alone.' He slipped his hand into the proffered lead apron and one minute later the machine was wheeled back out.

He picked up the wires for the cardiac monitor. There was no way electrodes could be fixed to this patient's chest—parts of his skin were missing. He motioned to Gabrielle. 'Help me sit him forward and I'll put these on his back. I want to try and keep an eye on his heart rate as well as his blood pressure.

She shook her head. 'No, wait a second.' She jogged out of the room and he could see her heading to the stairs. He kept an eye on his patient as one of the nurses came in with a check list. He scanned the list. There were twenty-one patients, including their injuries and current status.

'Where did the Chinese worker with a leg fracture go?'

The nurse looked at him anxiously. 'They took the rest of the patients to Princess Elizabeth's—it's one of the other private hospitals. It has a few specialist eye surgeons and an orthopaedist. Princess Gabrielle arranged it.' The nurse glanced around at the quiet chaos in the surrounding department. 'She was worried we wouldn't have enough theatres or staff.'

Sullivan nodded carefully. She'd triaged the patients as they'd come in. He'd been doing it at one end—and she'd been doing it at the other. It seemed that in emergency situations Gabrielle Cartier kept a clear and rational head. He ran his eyes down the list again. 'Okay, we seem to have the majority of patients with burns and explosive injuries.'

The nurse bit her bottom lip. 'Princess Gabrielle said you would be able to handle those. She's arranged for two plastic surgeons to join you. I think they're familiarising themselves with the theatre arrangements.'

'Perfect.' She really had thought of everything.

The door to the stairs swung open and Gabrielle jogged back towards them, her ponytail swinging madly. She had a sealed surgical pack in her hands that she waved at him.

'They do a lot of cardiac surgery here. They have proper packs in Theatre. These leads can go on the patient's back instead of their chest.'

Of course. They were in a state-of-the-art hospital. They probably had equipment that he'd not even seen yet.

They placed the leads on the patient's back as the chest X-ray was slid onto the light box by the radiographer. She didn't wait for Sullivan's diagnosis. 'Large penetrating injury to the right lung. No wonder his sats are poor. He has a pneumothorax.'

The radiographer was right. Sullivan just wasn't used to people reading his X-rays for him. He glanced at the monitor. 'If we have a theatre available I'd rather deal with the pneumothorax in there. It makes sense to be next to the anaesthetist when our next step is to remove what's causing the lung collapse and then deal with the burns.'

Gabrielle's dark eyes met his own. 'That'll be a long surgery.'

He nodded. 'It will.'

She could see her biting the inside of her cheek. 'What is it?'

'We have other patients who will require surgery. I think we'll have enough staff to have two teams. Do you want to triage the patients?'

Ah. That was it. He got it. She'd felt confident enough to categorise the patients and send them to the most appropriate hospital. But she wasn't a surgeon. She didn't want to step outside her field of expertise. It was up to him to prioritise the surgical cases.

'Absolutely.' He looked down at their clothes. 'And I guess we should both find a pair of scrubs.'

This time she smiled. She was used to him joking when they were at work together. In fact, this was the most normal things had felt between them in the last thirty or so hours. He felt like a fish out of water in the palace. Here? Even though he didn't know this hospital, this healthcare system or the staff, he felt much more at home.

And even though this was an emergency situation, Gabrielle seemed more relaxed too. Being a doctor was second nature to her. She could adapt to any situation. It brought out the best in her. It was her home too.

Even though they'd barely been there a day, she'd seemed fraught with tension in the palace. As he looked at everyone hurrying to and fro in the emergency department he leaned over and put his hand on her shoulder.

'I have no idea just how much you've done here, or how many promises you had to make to get these two hospitals to take the patients from the mines, but, Gabrielle, without these facilities a lot of these miners could have died.' He took a long slow breath. 'I think your negotiation skills will have to continue. Lots of the people affected will have a long road to recovery. I have no idea how the healthcare system works here, but you could have a tough time ahead.'

'Not as tough as these patients.' Her voice was firm and determined. 'Let me worry about that.' She gave him a soft smile. 'I'm just glad you were here, Sullivan. Today needs a trauma surgeon and a burns specialist and that's you. I know these patients are in safe hands. That's the most important thing in the world.' She gave a nod of her head. 'Now, check over the patients for me, then go to surgery. I'll see you later.'

He bent lower and brushed a tiny kiss on her cheek. 'Proud of you,' he whispered, and as he raised his head he saw her eyes glisten with unshed tears.

It was the first time he'd kissed her since they'd got there. For the briefest second he could see a million things flashing in her eyes. Attraction. Sorrow. Worry. Then he saw her suck in a breath and move away quickly.

It only took ten minutes to review the other patients with one of the nurses. 'This man next, he has full-thickness burns to twenty per cent of his body. I'll take him once I've finished with Mr Bahn. This patient goes to the other team; he has semi-thickness burns that will require cleaning and a skin graft. This lady, Arona Jibel, put her on the other team's list too. She has multiple small penetrating wounds that all need to be debrided.

Put a note she'll need X-rays in Theatre to make sure they've got everything. And this man with the hand injuries and burns to his thighs, I'll do him third. The two patients with facial injuries—cheeks and foreheads—put them on the list for the other team. I think Gabrielle said there are two plastic surgeons on that team. If I'm finished before them, I can take one of those patients.' The nurse nodded and scribbled notes furiously. Sullivan held out his hand towards her. 'And thank you. Everyone here today has been great. I know this isn't what you're used to.'

She gave him a smile and she shook his hand. 'Actually, it reminded me how much I liked to be challenged at work. I'd think I'd forgotten for a while. Now, get going, I'll organise everything else and make sure these patients are monitored.'

Sullivan glanced back out into the corridor and leaned back, stretching his back muscles. There was no sign of Gabrielle. But that was fine. For the next twelve hours he would probably be very busy.

The difference between the Gabrielle he saw here and the Gabrielle back in the palace had given him a lot to think about.

Fourteen hours later Sullivan finally left Theatre. Half of Gabrielle's personal palace staff had arrived at one point or another at the hospital. The director of St George's had been charm itself, and had invited them to use his own personal suite. But Gabrielle wanted to be near the patients that she considered under her care. She'd taken a quick car ride to Princess Elizabeth's and checked on the patients and staff there too.

A whole array of directors had arrived from the mining corporation. Gabrielle had directed her staff to deal with them. 'Find out contact information for all their workers—there's a huge variety of nationalities—and make sure the hospitals have the information they need. If we need translators, arrange that too.' She glanced at Franz Hindermann. 'There'll need to be an investigation into how this accident occurred. I have other priorities but I expect our government to act appropriately. Make sure the mining corporation know that they will be footing the bill for all expenses. *All expenses,*' she emphasised. 'They should have insurance to cover it—I'm not sure all their workers will. We'll talk about that later too.'

She'd finally managed to procure a pair of violet scrubs and a thick pair of socks. At least she felt comfortable here at work, but from the glances Franz shot her, he was far from happy.

'Shouldn't you change? The people of Mirinez will expect a statement from their Head of State. You can't do it looking like that.'

She glanced down and felt a little surge of anger.

'Why not? Their Head of State is a doctor. They should be proud of her.'

Sullivan's voice cut through everything.

She jumped to her feet and ran over to him. What she really wanted to do was wrap her arms around his neck but it was hardly the time or place. 'How are you? Is everything okay?'

He pulled his surgical hat from his ruffled hair. There were huge dark circles under his eyes. He looked exhausted. 'First case took longer than any of us thought. Mr Bahn arrested in Theatre. He's in ICU now. I've just checked on him again before I came down here. I've also spoke to the other surgical team about their patients.' He gave a weary smile. 'I have to say, for a bunch of plastic surgeons they've done a damn good job.'

She tipped her head to the side. 'You didn't think they would?'

He shrugged. 'I hoped. Most of these guys have spent the last few years performing cosmetic surgery. Breasts, noses, lips and liposuction.'

She shook her head. 'Nope. We have plenty of those too, but I demanded the doctors I knew had worked on skin and facial reconstructions. I thought they would be best.'

He gave her an appreciative smile. 'Then you were right. The two patients who needed facial surgery couldn't have got any better in the US. I'm impressed.'

'And I'm relieved,' she sighed. 'I'm just glad everything came together.' She held up her hands. 'Shouldn't we have a national disaster plan, where everything just falls into place?'

Sullivan threw back his head and laughed. He'd worked in enough countries and with enough organisations to know just how difficult those things were. 'Good luck with that. You're right, you should. In case of emergency, there should be an agreement between all healthcare providers in Mirinez that they'll play their part.' He shrugged. 'I don't expect them to do it for free, but when was the last time you had an emergency like this in Mirinez?'

Gabrielle glanced at Franz then Arun, who was standing by the door, and back to Franz again. 'I don't actually remember if we've ever had an emergency before.'

Franz frowned. 'There was some trouble at the harbour once. An accident when a boat capsized. There were around ten casualties.'

'And who looked after them?'

Franz looked a little embarrassed. 'Your father asked the French Prime Minister for help.'

Gabrielle couldn't help but let out an exasperated sigh. 'We need to do something about this.'

Then a horrible realisation swept over her. '*I need to do something about this.*'

Sullivan's arm slid around her waist. While the warmth and familiarity was instantly welcomed, a thousand other thoughts of country and duty pushed into her head. 'What you need to do—in fact, what *we* need to do—is get some sleep. I'm happy the patients are settled for now and we can check on them later.'

She didn't step away. Couldn't. She'd forgotten just how tired he looked. He'd been down a mine then on his feet in Theatre for the last fourteen hours. She was proving to be a terrible host.

'Of course, you're right. Let's go.'

Franz held up his hand. 'But what about the statement? The people will be expecting one.'

Sullivan's arm put a little pressure on her from behind, urging her down the corridor. 'Just write a press release,' he said over his shoulder.

Arun walked in front of them, holding open the door of one of the palace limousines. 'Arun waited too?' Sullivan asked.

She smiled. 'And Mikel. He went to Princess Elizabeth's to see if he could help—answering phones, wheeling patients about. He said he wanted to.'

Sullivan gave a strange kind of smile. 'It's amazing how a disaster can bring out qualities you hadn't noticed before.'

He leaned back in the seat, letting himself sink into the soft leather. His arm moved from her waist to curl around her shoulders. She followed his lead and leant her head against his chest, closing her eyes for a few seconds.

Next minute Arun was opening the door and the cool air swept around them. She rubbed her eyes and stepped out of the car, waiting for Sullivan.

The palace corridors were quiet. Half of the staff would no doubt be glued to the news channels and the other half would be answering phones and queries from all over the globe.

Her feet started to slow as she started to wonder if she should offer to go and help.

'No,' said Sullivan firmly.

She stared up at him from tired eyes. 'What do you mean, no?'

He kept her walking. 'You're not going to do anything else. You're going to rest. Take a few hours down time. Everything immediate has been dealt with.'

She knew he was right, but something inside her stomach coiled. 'But—'

He cut her off. 'But your staff haven't had a functioning Head of State in over a year. Do you think Andreas would have organised any emergency services? Would he have found other surgeons? Treated patients? Negotiated with the directors of the hospitals?'

Fatigue rested heavily on her shoulders. 'No. But he isn't a doctor. He wouldn't have been able to think that way.'

Sullivan stopped outside her doorway. 'But would he have done *anything*?' The coil inside her stomach gave a little somersault.

She pushed open her door and looked inside. In her eyes, this room still belonged to her brother. It didn't feel like the most restful place to be—she'd spent most of last night tossing and turning.

She turned back to face Sullivan. His pale green eyes stood out against the dark night visible through her windows. 'Probably not,' she whispered.

She hesitated at the door again.

'What's wrong?' he asked.

She shook her head. 'I just don't want to sleep in there.'

He gave a half-smile. 'In that case, come with me.'

He slid his hand into hers. 'I can't promise you'll be safe.'

Her heart ached. He had no idea how her thoughts tumbled around her mind right now. One hint of impropriety, one mis-seen kiss and the weight of a nation that was currently around her neck would end up around Sullivan's too. She still hadn't heard from Andreas. She still didn't know why he'd left. Could it have been the pressure to start a family? They'd never discussed his family plans. But as soon as he'd married, there had been constant press speculation about a pregnancy—an heir to the throne.

In the blink of an eye the same could happen to her. Every sighting of her with a man would result in hints of an engagement then a wedding. Then the pressure to have a baby, to continue the line of succession for Mirinez.

How could she contemplate putting all of that on Sullivan? There were already tiny shadows behind his eyes. He hadn't told her everything. She knew that. But she respected his right to privacy. The press wouldn't.

She looked down the empty corridor. She felt entirely selfish. And so physically tired. But still it was as though every cell in her body just ached for him. She pushed everything else aside. Gave him a smile. 'I think I will be. I could probably sleep standing up right now.' He raised his eyebrows and she added, 'I'd just rather do it next to you.'

He opened the door to his apartments. The bed was right in the middle of the room, the dark windows looking out over the city below. He pulled his scrub top over his head and kicked off his shoes before he was even halfway across the room. She sat down on the edge of the bed and wriggled out of her scrub trousers and pulled off her borrowed shoes and socks, hesitating at the bottom of her top.

A soft T-shirt landed sideways on her shoulder. 'Here, have this,' he said as he climbed into bed, wearing only his black jockey shorts. This wasn't exactly how she'd expected to spend her first night in Sullivan's bed, but for now it just felt right.

'Thanks,' she said, swiftly swapping the scrub top for the T-shirt and crawling into bed next to him.

He held out his arm and she put her head on his chest, her arm resting across his body.

For the first time since she'd returned home she felt relieved.

This was exactly how things were supposed to be.

CHAPTER EIGHT

It was the ideal way to wake up. A warm body
next to his, their limbs intertwined, and soft
lemon-scented hair under his nose.

Once his eyes had flickered open he really
didn't want to move.

He glanced at the clock. It was only six a.m.
So far he'd seen one a.m., two a.m. and five a.m.
Thankfully he'd missed three a.m. and four a.m.
Last night had been a good night and Gabrielle's
steady breathing had definitely played a part in
that. It was likely that Gabrielle's day was due to
start any minute. He would dearly love to wake
her up with the promise that had been hovering
between them since they'd first met.

His *body* wanted him to wake her that way.

He gave a little groan as she shifted next to him
and laid her palm on his bare chest. He wasn't
quite sure how Gabrielle wanted to play this.

The palace staff would be looking for her any
minute. Would Princess Gabrielle want to be
found in his apartments, wearing only a T-shirt
and her underwear? He didn't think so.

He gave her a gentle shake. 'Gabrielle, wake

up. We have patients to check on and you have a country to run.'

She made a comfortable little noise as she snuggled closer, her fingers brushing the hairs on his chest. 'It can't be time yet. It just can't.'

He smiled. The temptation to stay here was too strong. Things were changing. A few days ago he'd thought he was going to have a harmless fling with a colleague. He hadn't contemplated anything else.

But circumstances had changed. For both of them.

The attraction between them was still strong. He would happily act on it in the blink of an eye. But Gabrielle wasn't just thinking about herself now. Everything she did would be examined and watched. He didn't want to make the front-page news in Mirinez. He didn't want her criticised or judged because of a casual relationship.

It was clear Gabrielle was already going to have to bear the brunt for the work her brother had ignored. He'd abdicated just as things were about to come to a head—that much was clear.

Her soft hair tickled under his nose and she moved her leg, brushing his thigh.

He groaned out loud.

She sat up in bed. 'What time is it? Oh, no. They'll be looking for me.'

He smiled. Her hair was mussed up and one

cheek showed a crease from the pillow. 'That's what I thought. That's why I woke you.'

She swung her legs around the edge of the bed then paused, her dark eyes fixing on his. 'You were pretty amazing yesterday. Did I even thank you?'

'You don't need to thank me. I'm a doctor, it's what I do. But I thought you were pretty amazing too. We make a good team.'

Her smile reached her eyes as she nodded. 'You're right, we do.' She sighed and ran her fingers through her hair, trying to tame it. 'I'll need to check up on what's happened with the directors of the mine. I'll probably need to give an update to Parliament.' She stood up and walked across the room. His pale T-shirt outlined her figure in the early morning light. 'And then I'll meet you back at the hospital and help review the patients.'

He pushed himself up in the bed. 'You won't need to do that. I'm sure there are enough doctors at the two hospitals who can help me review the patients.'

'You don't know what the private hospitals can be like. Some doctors only like to see their own fee-paying patients.'

'Well, I didn't meet any of them last night. Maybe the fact that Princess Gabrielle was front and centre in the whole affair helped them find their civic sense?'

She shook her head. 'I'm fairly sure that the cold light of day and the arrival of the hospital accountants will mean that today will mainly be about finances.'

He slid out of bed and started to search through his backpack for some suitable clothes. 'Then I'm sure you can find a way to deal with it. This was an emergency situation. It might be the first, but you have to plan ahead. Give the task to Parliament to deal with.'

She looked thoughtful then walked back over to him, putting one hand on top of his arm and reaching the other up to touch his cheek. 'I'm sorry,' she whispered. 'This wasn't exactly how I imagined us spending the night together.'

He shook his head. 'Me neither.'

She licked her lips. It was almost as if she was trying to stop the words that came to her lips. 'Then let me make it up to you. How about dinner tonight? We haven't had a chance to spend much time together.'

'I like the sound of that.'

She stood on tiptoe and planted a soft kiss on his lips. 'Then let's make it a date.' She grinned as she spun around and headed to the door. 'And dress appropriately, Dr Darcy!'

It was odd. She'd worked with the guy at close quarters for two weeks. She was still sorry that their night at the bar had been curtailed and waking up in his arms this morning had felt much more comfortable than it should have.

The day had gone quickly. There had been legal requirements, more agreements to sign, a meeting with Parliament, then she'd shared the rest of the day between the two hospitals. By the time she'd got to the first, Sullivan had reviewed all his patients and gone to the second hospital to help with communication with the Chinese patient.

He'd been right. The hospital doctors had cancelled their theatre lists and reviewed all the accident victims. It was only the finance departments that had a whole host of queries, but she'd expected those.

She was only just beginning to get a handle on exactly how much work her brother had left behind. He still hadn't answered any calls or emails. He must have heard about the explosion in the mine but he still hadn't called home. It was probably just as well, because right now most of what she'd say to him couldn't be repeated.

She adjusted the straps on her black dress and gave a wriggle. She hadn't quite got used to wearing formal clothes again. Yesterday the scrubs had been a relief. And when she'd opened her wardrobe tonight to find something to wear to dinner, she'd felt strangely nervous.

The thoughts of the press finding out about Sullivan being in the palace with her still made her nervous.

Any man who decided to be with Princess Gabrielle would need to know what he was getting into. Every inch of his life would be exposed to the press. Sullivan could be sparky. Sullivan could be fun. His doctor side was compassionate and expertly efficient. But there was part of him that was private.

She needed to tread carefully. When she'd woken this morning, for a few seconds she'd felt nothing but bliss. But as soon as she'd opened the door and walked down the corridor to her apartments her royal life had been back, front and foremost.

Something was blossoming between them, that much was clear. That had been the impetus for tonight's invitation. She'd spoken on instinct, wanting to reach out and find out what came next.

Later her stomach had churned. Her emotions had cooled and rational thoughts had filled her brain. A tiny little seed was taking root. She liked him. She liked him a *lot*. Make the wrong move and Sullivan could be scared off by the press.

He'd served two tours of duty. He probably wasn't the kind of guy to be scared off by a few photographers or articles. He didn't strike her as that kind of guy at all. But she just didn't know. And she was scared.

Scared enough to have spoken at length to Arun today. Everything about tonight was to be entirely private. Sullivan had insisted on organising everything, but she had made sure there would be no whisper about what they were doing.

Her black dress with sequins around the V-shaped neckline was a favourite. Anji, one of the palace ladies-in-waiting, gave her an approving smile. 'Your Majesty should wear your mother's necklace with that.'

Gabrielle gave a little start. She'd completely forgotten about the family jewels. In a way, she was surprised that Andreas's wife hadn't taken them all with her.

'Where are they?'

Anji smiled. 'In the main safe. The diamond drop necklace would look perfect with that dress.'

Gabrielle stared at her reflection for a second. Anji was right. It would look perfect. But opening the safe and wearing the family jewels would be another step towards being the ruler, remaining the Princess. Her stomach flipped over. She still hadn't got used to the idea. This all just seemed so unreal. Almost as if she were living someone else's life.

Her mouth was dry. 'Okay, would you tell Arun I'd like to access the safe?'

It was ridiculous that she should be nervous. She'd already seen the administrative work that needed to be done for Mirinez. She hadn't even questioned that there were treaties to sign, deals to negotiate. But this was different. This was personal.

A few moments later Arun appeared behind her and led her down the corridor to the family safe. He gave her a nod. As Head of Security he knew every item in the safe. She sucked in a breath as it was swung open.

'I half expected the family jewels to be gone,' she joked.

Arun glanced over her shoulder. 'Some of them were. I had to make sure they were returned.'

Her eyes widened. 'You mean…'

He slid out a tray from the safe. 'Let's not talk about it now. The diamond drop necklace? This is the one that you wanted, is it not?'

The necklace was in a black velvet box. He flipped it open to reveal the ten-carat sparkling jewel set in yellow gold. Her hands shook as she lifted it from the case. 'Yes, this is it. Thank you.'

Her breath caught in her throat. At the back of the safe, in two glass cases, sat two crowns. One for a Prince, with a heavy gold underlay and adorned with rubies, diamonds and emeralds, and one for a Princess, a more elegant version, mainly with diamonds.

Arun caught her glance. 'Mr Hindermann is already discussing potential dates for the neighbouring Heads of State to attend the official ceremony.'

A little chill ran down her spine. She couldn't hold off any longer. Her brother's abdication had been announced as soon as they'd been able to contact her. The citizens of Mirinez would expect the official ceremony soon—any delay would raise questions.

She gave a little nod of her head. 'That will be all, Arun. Thank you for this and thank you for tonight. I trust the arrangements are in place?'

Arun gave a quick nod.

She gave a nervous smile. 'Good. I'll let you know when I want to return the necklace to the safe.'

'As you wish.' He sealed the safe and disappeared discreetly. He would appear again soon. He said that Sullivan had discussed tonight's arrangements with him.

Sullivan was standing outside her royal apartment, wearing a pair of black dress trousers and a white shirt. 'I wondered where you were,' he said as she walked down the corridor towards him. His gaze swept up and down her appreciatively, settling finally on the jewel at her throat. 'Wow, you could take someone's eye out with that.'

She burst out laughing. 'Who taught you your manners?'

He laughed too. 'Just calling it like I see it.' Then he shook his head. 'My father would be horrified if he heard that.'

Something passed across his face. It was a fleeting expression but one that she'd seen for a few seconds a couple of times before.

She reached up and touched his arm. 'How long is it since you lost your father?'

It was almost as if she could see the shutters falling behind his eyes. 'Three years.' He waved his hand. 'It's been a while. Now, about dinner.'

She bit her tongue. It was clear he didn't want to discuss this. It made her curious. What did he have to hide? For the most part Sullivan seemed like a straight-down-the-line kind of guy. But, in truth, he hadn't revealed that much about himself. Their first two weeks together had been in part intense work and intense flirtation. The last couple of days had been chaotic. She hadn't even had a chance to ask him what he thought of Mirinez, let alone fathom out where they were with each other.

She gave a conciliatory nod. 'Okay, then what about dinner? It could be I'm all dressed up with nowhere to go.'

One of his eyebrows quirked upwards. It made her laugh. 'I have plans,' he said as he swept an arm around her waist and started along the corridor.

'Where are we going?' She was curious. It had been a few years since she'd visited any of the restaurants in Mirinez. She didn't even know which ones still existed.

He took her down the main staircase. Arun was waiting at the front door with the car engine running. As they slid into the back Sullivan gave her a smile. 'We've had to make special arrangements.'

'What arrangements?' She touched the necklace at her throat nervously. 'Is this about the necklace?'

Sullivan laughed. 'No, this is about the *person* wearing the necklace. You're Head of State now, Princess Gabrielle. It means you get to book out a whole restaurant for yourself—or, at least, I do.'

She sat upright as the car moved along the palace driveway. 'Really? I hadn't thought of that.' She frowned. 'I can't remember that happening with my parents.'

Sullivan gave her a careful look. 'I think Arun might have re-evaluated some safety aspects of your current role.'

'But I spent most of yesterday in the hospital, seeing patients. I have to be able to move around.' She gave a simple answer, but her stomach gave a few flips. Arun had taken her request for complete privacy seriously.

Sullivan nodded. 'I get that. But didn't you notice how many black-suited men were in your vicinity yesterday?'

She sagged back against the comfortable leather seats. 'Well, no. I didn't even think about it.' And she hadn't. She been so busy thinking about other things.

Sullivan held up his hands. 'That's because you don't have to. Arun does.'

It was almost like a heavy weight settling on her shoulders. If she thought about it hard enough, she could remember the security staff always being around—she'd just assumed they were there to help, it had been an all-hands-on-deck kind of day—she just hadn't realised they had actually been there to guard *her.*

'The world has changed since you were a child, Gabrielle. Arun has to take so many other factors into consideration now. Nothing is secret. One tweet and the world knows where you are.'

She gulped. Sullivan had been in the military. He was probably a lot more familiar with all the security stuff than she was.

But what about the privacy stuff? The press?

She looked out of the window at the darkening sky. It was almost as if Sullivan could sense the turmoil of thoughts racing through her brain and he slid his hand over hers and intertwined their fingers.

She closed her eyes for a second and took a deep breath. She couldn't remember ever feeling like this before, experiencing a real connection with someone that she wanted to take further. She'd had teenage crushes and her heart had been broken a few times along the way, but for the last few years she'd been focused on her work. The couple of passing flings she'd had didn't count. This was the first relationship that actually felt real. Actually felt as if it could go somewhere. But at a time like this was it even worth thinking about?

The car pulled up outside a glass-fronted restaurant that Gabrielle didn't recognise. The street was in one of the most exclusive parts of Chabonnex. Sullivan got out of the car and greeted the maître d' in Italian before holding his hand out towards her.

She'd hardly had a chance to even stop and think but right now everything was paling in comparison to the handsome guy before her. Did he realise how well he filled out those clothes? The white shirt was a blessing, defining all the muscles on his arms and chest.

Then she paused for a second—had Sullivan lost weight? He looked a little leaner than before. But the thought disappeared as the streetlamp next to them highlighted his tanned skin and the twinkle in his pale green eyes. The one thing that made her heart stop in her chest was his smile.

He was looking at her as if she was the only woman in the world and that smile was entirely for her.

Her heart gave a little flutter and she slid from the car, putting her hand into his. The restaurant was empty and the maître d' led them upstairs to a starlit terrace. Arun and his security team positioned themselves as unobtrusively as possible.

Sullivan pulled out her chair and seated her then settled opposite her. 'So, tonight, Princess, we're having Italian.' He held up the wine list. 'What would you prefer?'

She waved her hand. The night air was mild and there was a heater burning next to them to ward off any unexpected chill. There was something nice about eating outside after the last few days of constantly being surrounded by walls. The soft music from the restaurant drifted out around them. 'Since my last glass of wine came from the bar in Paris…' she leaned forward and whispered '…where—don't tell anyone—the wine was on tap. I'll be happy with whatever you choose.'

He gave a nod and ordered from the maître d'. A few minutes later their glasses were filled, their food order was taken and she sat back and relaxed.

Although the restaurant was empty, there were still people in the street below them. It was nice, watching the world go by.

'Happy?' Sullivan asked as he held up his glass towards her.

She clinked her glass against his. 'You realise there'll be a scandal if I'm caught doing this. I'm quite sure it will be considered unladylike and won't be becoming for the Head of State.'

He shrugged. 'It could be worse—it could be a bottle of beer. Anyway, I thought you would live by your own rules, not the ones you inherit.'

She opened her mouth to reply automatically, then stopped. Coming back here, suddenly everything felt so ingrained into her. Her childhood memories of her mother and father. Discussions about conduct and acceptable behaviour. Of course, she'd never felt the same pressure that her brother, Andreas, had been under—it had always been expected that he would fulfil his role. And she was quite sure that her lifestyle had never been as strict as some of her royal counterparts in other European countries.

But these rules were still deep inside her. Almost as if they ran through her veins. She sat her glass down carefully. 'Being Head of State is a big responsibility.'

'I didn't say it wasn't. You seem to be doing an admirable job already.' Sullivan was so matter-of-fact, as if it was all entirely obvious. 'But who is here to tell you how to live your life? Your brother certainly isn't. You're a good person, Gabrielle, and you'll do your best to sort out the mess he's left behind, but you don't need to lose yourself in the process.'

She sucked in a breath to speak but changed her mind, picked her glass up again and took a hefty swallow.

She'd spent the last few years completely under the radar—not being a princess at all. If any one of her colleagues had started a conversation with her about not conforming to the rules of being a doctor, she would have happily had that discussion. She would have enjoyed the debate.

But this was so much more personal.

The waiter appeared and placed their entrées in front of them. Sullivan smiled and took the wine from the cooler and topped up her glass. She ran her fingers up and down the stem of the wine glass, contemplating his words. But Sullivan wasn't finished. He continued, 'I thought you royal children had something inbuilt into you all—a kind of thing that always said, *This could be me.* Life changes constantly, Gabrielle. You're a doctor. You know that better than most. Accidents happen. People get sick. Surely you must have known this could always have been a possibility?'

She shook her head. 'But I didn't want this. I didn't ask to be born into this life. I've spent the last few years running away from it—keeping my head down and doing the kind of work that I wanted to do.'

'And you can't do that now?'

She stared at her entrée. The jungle seemed a million miles away. Right now it felt as if she would never get back there, never get to lead a team on another TB mission, never to get dance in her tent late at night.

'I'm not sure I can,' she whispered.

Sullivan reached over and squeezed her hand as a shiver went down her spine. Saying the words out loud was scary. They'd been dancing around in her head from the second Arun and the rest of the security team had approached her in Paris.

She met Sullivan's gaze. 'I feel as if my life has been stolen from me.' She closed her eyes for a second. 'And I feel terrible about the thoughts I'm having about my brother.'

'Is he still incommunicado?'

She nodded her head. 'Why can't he even have the courtesy to have a conversation with me? I know things happen. But it wasn't as if anything in particular did happen here. Andreas left. He chose to leave. He could have waited until I was back. He could have told me he didn't want to rule. We could have come to some…arrangement.'

Sullivan took a sip of his wine. 'And what kind of arrangement could that be? Oh, just let me work for the next ten years, Andreas, and then I'll come back and take over from you?'

Indignation swept through her. 'What's so wrong about that? At least then there would have been plans, a chance to think ahead—anything but leave the principality in the state it is now.'

Sullivan picked up his fork. 'Could there be anything else going on?'

'You mean besides his wife?'

Sullivan frowned. 'You said he'd emailed you while we were in the jungle. It's obvious he hasn't looked after things well these last few years.'

'What are you implying?'

He looked her straight in the eye. 'Could Andreas be depressed, for example?'

She was stunned. It hadn't even crossed her mind. Not for a second. She had just been so angry with him for disappearing and not answering any calls, texts or emails.

She picked up her fork and started toying with her food. 'I have no idea. We haven't been close these last few years. His wife…his wife has been his biggest influence.'

Sullivan must have picked up on her tone. The

edges of his lips turned upwards. 'You don't like her much, do you?'

'I don't have much in common with a TV actress whose idea of a humanitarian act is to donate her lipstick to the nearest charity.'

Sullivan almost choked on his food. 'Okay, then, I'll give you that one.'

Gabrielle finally managed to put some of the delicious smoked salmon into her mouth. After a few months in the jungle, some burgers at the bar in Paris and quick hospital sandwich last night and today, it had been a long time since she'd tasted something so good.

She leaned back in her chair and gave a little groan. 'Can we come back here every night?'

Sullivan nodded. His plate was half-empty. He was obviously already enjoying his food. 'Fine with me. I think Arun might have something to say about it, though.' He leaned forward and whispered, 'I think we caused him a bit of a headache tonight.'

She smiled and looked around, taking the time to pick out some of the familiar sights of the capital city. The cathedral, the old monastery, the brick distillery. All of these had been part of her daily commute to private school.

She could feel the tension start to leave her shoulders. Thinking about Mirinez generally tied her up in knots. She'd been so on edge since she'd got back she hadn't taken the time to think about the things she liked about being here.

The food. The people. The weather.

Too much of her time had been spent on all the things that made her insides twist and turn. She sipped at her wine as she tried to relax a little. The uptight person she'd been these last few days wasn't normal for Gabrielle at all, even when she was working as a doctor in a time of crisis.

The waiter came and magically swapped their plates and the smell of her langoustine ravioli made her stomach growl. Sullivan smiled and picked up his fork. 'Feeling better yet?'

She took her first mouthful. 'Yes. I'd forgotten how good food like this tastes.' She gave her stomach a pat. 'If we eat here every night I'll need a major workout plan.'

'You mean besides running a country?'

She nodded as his phone beeped. He pulled it from his pocket, looked at it and stuffed it back. Her heart gave a few thuds against her chest. 'The hospital? Is there a problem?'

He looked amused. 'No. Not at all. It was Gibbs.'

'Gibbs?' The name of their co-ordinator at Doctors Without Borders jolted her back to reality. Sullivan had agreed to come with her Mirinez—to offer her support—but she had forgotten there would always be a time limit.

'We've just got here. He can't be trying to send you on another mission already?'

Sullivan shrugged and didn't answer.

'He is?' She was indignant on his behalf. She knew he'd come straight from one mission to join hers. They'd only just arrived in Paris before they'd come here and then been thrown straight into the mine accident.

'You need a break. You need some down time.' Then she shook her head at the irony. 'And you haven't exactly managed to get any here.'

'It doesn't really matter. I like working.'

'But there are rules about these things. We're supposed to have a certain amount of time between our missions. You've already stepped into an emergency once, there can't be another already.'

He raised one eyebrow. 'Can't there?'

She put down her fork. It didn't matter how delicious the food in front of her, for some reason she'd just lost her appetite. 'What does he want you to do?'

Sullivan finished another mouthful of food. 'I don't know. I haven't phoned him back. And I won't—not yet, anyway. I want to review the patients I've operated on. I might take the miner with the injured hand back to Theatre. I'm worried about contractures. I'll need to stay for at least...' he paused for a second '...a week or so.'

She gulped. 'That's not enough of a break. Plus, you're actually working.'

'Not all the time.' There was a twinkle in his eye now. A little pulse of adrenaline surged through her body.

She picked up her fork and played with her food. That glint was taking her places she couldn't go anywhere in public. She'd never met anyone who could do that to her with just one look, just one smile.

'Do you ever have a holiday, Sullivan?' she sighed. 'I get the impression maybe not.'

He took a sip of his wine. 'The last holiday I had was around four years ago. My father decided we should do some touring. We spent three weeks on the road. Started in San Francisco, then went down to Los Angeles, across to Las Vegas then on into Utah and some of the national parks.' He gave a sad kind of smile. 'We hired a camper, and after the first week of sleeping in the camper my father could hardly walk. He said it was hotels all the way after that.' He gave a sudden laugh.

'What is it?'

'That was until we hit Utah and the national parks. Oh, no, then he didn't want to stay in a hotel. Then he wanted to camp and stare up at the starry sky at night.'

'And did you?'

Sullivan waved his hand. 'Yeah. We bought the

whole kit and caboodle. I've never felt ground so hard in my life and I've never seen rain like it. And by the next day? *Neither* of us could walk.'

Gabrielle started laughing. It was clear from the way that he talked he'd had a good relationship with his father. She wished she could have seen them together. But as just as quickly as the joy had appeared in Sullivan's eyes they shadowed over again.

She'd seen that look before, when he'd mentioned casually that he hadn't had a chance to pack up his father's things back home in Oregon. It hadn't seemed significant at the time, but now she was getting to know him a little better it felt a little off. Working with Sullivan had shown her he was incredibly organised.

But even now he didn't seem entirely anxious to go home. There had been no pre-booked flight to Oregon to cancel when she'd asked him to accompany her. And she got the feeling if he hadn't been with her now, he might have answered Gibbs's text about the next mission. How could she phrase the question that was burning inside her?

She never got the chance because Sullivan nodded towards the old-fashioned picture house opposite the restaurant. It had a small poster on either side of the main doors advertising the latest action movie.

'What's with the place across the street?'

She smiled. 'The Regal? It's a picture-house based in one of the oldest buildings in Mirinez. There have been lots of attempts to modernise it—all of them resisted.' She couldn't help but let out a laugh. She'd witnessed some of the fierce arguments about 'dragging things into the twenty-first century', but she had fond memories of the picture house. Even looking at it now spread a little warm glow through her body.

'And they've all failed?' Sullivan looked interested.

'More or less. The electrics and plumbing have been modernised. The screen has been changed, but it's still like walking into an old theatre rather than one of those cinema complexes. The chairs are original—a tiny bit uncomfortable and covered in dark red velvet.'

'Just one screen?'

'Just the one. And each film only plays for a week so if you miss it, you miss it.'

'It's kinda quaint.'

She laughed again. 'There's a word I never thought I hear on Sullivan Darcy's lips.'

'Quaint? My dad used it, quite a lot actually. He must have picked it up when we stayed in England for a while.'

He tapped his fingers on the table. 'I guess if

we want to see the latest action movie we'd better go in the next few days, then.'

Gabrielle started to nod and then rolled her eyes. 'We might have a problem.'

'Why?'

She held out her hands. 'Look at this place. You said Arun had to book the whole place out so we could come to dinner. If he tried to book the cinema out for just us, the rest of Mirinez would probably riot.'

'How about a private showing—could we arrange that?'

She sighed. 'Probably. But then we'd need to go in the middle of the night or first thing in the morning. It kind of takes the joy out of going to the cinema. You know, filing into your seat with your giant bag of popcorn and waiting for the lights to go down and hear the theme tune before the adverts start. There'd be no atmosphere.'

Sullivan thought for a few seconds. 'What if we go incognito?'

'What?' She hadn't even thought of that.

'You never did anything like that as a kid?'

'Well, sure I did. But we only had one security guy and he was really for Andreas, not for me. I used to sneak out to places all the time.'

'So…sneak out someplace with me?' All of a sudden she felt around fifteen again. It was the oddest thrill. Sneaking out somewhere with the bad boy. But, then, Sullivan wasn't really a bad boy, was he? It was just the way he said those words, almost as if it were a challenge.

And she loved a challenge.

She glanced over at the cinema. She'd love to go back there. She would. But as she watched the people milling around outside, a horrible black cloud of responsibility settled on her shoulders.

It was automatic. The enormous list of things that still needed to be dealt with started running through her head. 'I'd love to, but I still need to meet the owners of the mine, I need to check a trade agreement with another country, there's dispute over a part of our boundary—our fishermen haven't apparently been following EU fishing regulations—there are issues around some of our exports. We have applications from six major new businesses that want to invest in Mirinez—'

'Whoa!' Sullivan held up his hand and stood up.

The background music had changed to something a little more familiar.

'What?' She looked around.

He turned the palm of his hand, extending it out towards her. 'Give me Gabrielle back, please.'

She frowned with confusion. 'What do you mean?'

He was giving her a knowing kind of smile. 'I

had her. I had her right there with me, then you just flipped back into princess mode.'

A little chill spread over her skin. He was right. She had. One second she'd been enjoying dinner with Sullivan, contemplating some fun, and the next? She'd been sucked back into the wave of responsibility that felt as if it could suffocate her.

Tears prickled in her eyes. But Sullivan kept his voice light, almost teasing. 'When Gabrielle hears this tune, there's only one thing she can do.'

The beat of Justin Timberlake filled the air around her. From the expression on Sullivan's face it was clear he was remembering their first meeting—when he'd caught her dancing around the tent in Narumba.

'How can any girl resist JT?' he asked again.

'How can any girl resist Sullivan Darcy?' she countered as she slid her hand into his.

The security staff seemed to have miraculously disappeared into the walls. After a few seconds it was easy to feel the beat and start to relax a little. Sullivan pulled her a little closer.

'I thought you didn't dance?' She smirked as the heat of his body pressed up against hers. Apart from the night she'd lain in his arms, this was the first time since Paris she'd really been in a place she wanted to be.

'I thought you needed to let your hair down a little,' he said huskily. 'Remember what it is to have some fun.'

She swung her head. 'But my hair is down,' she argued, as her curls bounced around her shoulders.

'Is it?' he asked as he swung her round and dipped her.

She squealed, laughing, her arms slipping up and fastening around his neck. He held her there for a second, his mouth just inches from hers. She glanced up at his dark hair, running a finger along the edges. 'This is the longest I've seen your hair. Is that a little kink? Does your normal buzz cut hide curls?' She was teasing. She couldn't help it.

This was the kind of life she wanted to live. She wanted to be free to work hard during the day and laugh, joke and flirt her way with a man who made her heart sing through the nights.

He swung her back up, so close her breasts pressed against his chest. 'Now, that, my lovely lady, would be telling. Isn't a guy supposed to have some secrets?'

She wrinkled her nose as a little wave of guilt swept through her. 'I thought we were kind of finished with secrets.'

He waved his hands as he kept them swaying to the beat of the song. 'Princess Schmincess.'

She blinked. 'Did you really just say that?'

'Say what?' This time he was teasing her. And she liked it. She ran her hands down the front of his chest.

'I think you've been holding out on me.'

He spun her around again. 'Really?'

'Really. You never demonstrated these dance moves in Narumba.'

She was trying not to concentrate too closely on those clear green eyes of his. The twinkle that they held practically danced across her skin. And that sexy smile of his was making her want to take actions entirely unsuitable for a public terrace.

He slowed his movements a little and traced his finger gently down her cheek. 'Maybe I was saving them for a private show.'

She groaned out loud. 'Stop it. I've got security guards around. If you keep talking to me like this we're going to have to skip dessert.'

He leaned down and whispered in her ear. 'I've always thought dessert was overrated.'

His lips met hers. For a few seconds her brain completely cleared. Tonight had been almost perfect. It was like some make-believe date. Dinner, wine, dancing and…

His hands tangled through her hair as he teased her with his lips and tongue. She didn't want to break the connection—she didn't even want to breathe. Any second now she might start seeing stars.

Sullivan Darcy knew how to kiss. He knew how to hold a woman and cradle her body next to his. He kissed her lips, down her neck and along to her collarbone. Then just as her mouth was hungry for more he met her again, head on. His smell was wrapping around her, clean, with a hint of musk, or maybe it was just the pheromones—because right now she was pretty sure the air was laced with them.

His hand moved from her hair to her waist, sliding upwards, his palm covering her breast. Every part of her body reacted. Every one of her senses was on fire. And there was an instant reciprocal effect from his body.

A sudden gust of wind swept past them.

She jumped back, breathless and trying to regain control. There saw a dark shape shuffle back somewhere inside the restaurant. She felt her face flush. The restaurant staff and security staff would just have witnessed their moment of passion.

She glanced back to their table, the unfinished wine and plates still waiting to be collected. People were chatting on the street below.

For a few seconds she'd been in her own little bubble with Sullivan Darcy. She didn't need a reality check. Didn't *want* a reality check.

So she did the only thing that seemed entirely rational.

She grabbed his hand. 'Let's go.'

CHAPTER NINE

THEY'D STUMBLED BACK to his apartments instead of hers. It seemed that Gabrielle wasn't comfortable in the royal apartments.

The morning sunrise was beautiful. From here Sullivan had part view of the mountain covered in patches of green and part view of the city beneath them, all swathed in oranges, pinks and purples.

It had been a long time since he'd had the time to watch the sunrise. And he'd never done it next to a woman like Gabrielle.

For the first time in a long time the night hadn't drawn out, like a continuing loop. He'd actually slept a little. Yes, his brain had still spun endlessly round and round, but there had been periods of calm. Periods of quiet. It seemed Gabrielle was a good influence on him.

She was sleeping peacefully now, the white sheets tangled around her body. Her brown hair was fanned across the pillow and for once her forehead was smooth and not furrowed with worry. From the second they'd reached Mirinez her beautiful face had been marred by a frown that he'd only seen once the whole time they'd worked together.

This was the way she should look. This was the Gabrielle he'd first met a few weeks ago. The woman he'd spent last night with.

His stomach curled a little. Part of him wished the Princess part and Mirinez had never happened. He'd liked it better when she'd just been Gabrielle Cartier, medic from Doctors Without Borders. A girl with great legs, even better shorts, a killer dance rhythm and sexy as hell.

Here in Mirinez Gabrielle seemed coated in layers. Last night had been about trying to peel them all back and let her have a little fun.

And, boy, had they had fun.

He'd spent the last three years only having short-term flings. When he'd first met Gabrielle, his brain had pushed her firmly into that category. But from first sight his body had reacted in a way it hadn't before. At just a glance, a smile, the spark from a touch, it knew. Gabrielle could never be a fling.

Last night had confirmed that in a way he could never have predicted. He could stay in this position, watching her sleep, for ever.

But the dark clouds were still circling above his head. Right now, Gabrielle was like a ray of bright sunshine trying to stream through. If he could believe the intensity of these emotions—if he wanted to act on them—he had to pull himself out of this fog. For the first time in three years he was actually starting to feel something. For the first time he was starting to question—wouldn't it be so much better to actually *feel* again?

There was a shuffling outside the door. Sullivan sat up in bed, frowning to listen a little closer. There were low voices.

He swung his legs out of bed and grabbed a T-shirt, opening the door of the bedroom. Franz, the palace advisor, was outside. 'Dr Darcy, I have a message for Princess Gabrielle and I couldn't find her in her apartments.'

Sullivan nodded. He was sure the whole palace knew exactly where she was. 'Do you want me to get her for you?'

Franz gave a brief nod of his head.

Sullivan closed the door again and crossed over to the bed, sitting on the edge and putting his hand on Gabrielle's bare shoulder. He gave her a gentle shake.

'Gabrielle? Wake up. Franz is looking for you. They have a message.'

Her dark eyes flickered open. It took her a few seconds to orientate herself. 'I fell asleep?' she asked, as she pushed herself up.

'Nope. I just kidnapped you and held you hostage.'

She pulled the sheet up to cover her breasts as she tried to untangle her legs. 'Oh, no.'

'What?'

'I've got no clothes.' She looked down at the floor. Her black dress was lying rumpled across the carpet, her bra hung from the arm of a chair, and as for her underwear...

Sullivan walked to the cupboard and tossed her a T-shirt. 'This is getting to be a habit. Maybe you should move some clothes in here.'

She looked a little startled by the comment. She pulled the T-shirt over her head and looked around the room again, colour flooding her cheeks as she picked up her dress and bra. 'Give me a pair of your jockey shorts too.'

He laughed as she scrambled into the shorts. 'Don't you have a robe—a dressing gown—in here?'

Sullivan shook his head. 'Why on earth would I need one of those?'

'To let me keep a bit of dignity?'

It was clear she was feeling tetchy. He walked through the bathroom and ran the tap, washing his face and hands, trying to wake up a little more. He flicked the switch on the shower to let it heat up. Coffee. He would find some coffee, then arrange to go back down to the hospital and review the patients.

Gabrielle appeared at the door, looking pale, a newspaper clutched in her hand.

'What is it?'

She lifted up the Italian broadsheet so he could see the headline.

He flinched.

Princess Gabrielle's affair with Delinquent Doc

He snatched the paper and started to read. Speaking Italian was different from reading it, but he could easily understand the gist of the article.

The trouble was, no matter what the article said, the picture told a thousand words. It was of the two of them on the terrace last night. They were locked together, his hand on her breast, her arms around his neck. There was no mistaking where the night was going.

He held up the paper, trying to temper the anger that was rising in his stomach. 'What's this about anyway? We're two consenting adults—we can do whatever we want.'

'Keep reading.' Her voice had a little tremor.

Sullivan's mobile started ringing. They both turned their heads, but he ignored it. He kept reading.

It was a hatchet job. It questioned Gabrielle's

suitability to be Head of State. It questioned her competence. There was nothing accurate in the article. It didn't even mention the fact she was a doctor and had worked for Doctors Without Borders for the last few years, or the work she'd done to help stop the spread of TB.

As for the 'Delinquent Doc', it seemed that no one knew Sullivan Darcy had served in the US forces. There was no mention that he'd just helped out with a national emergency in Mirinez. No. All that was mentioned was a minor caution he'd received as a teenager from the police—something that had only ever been reported on in the local paper back in his home town. There wouldn't even be a record of it any more.

There was one final press comment.

Is this the man Princess Gabrielle will marry?

It was like a punch to the stomach. One date. One kiss. One night in bed—and the press didn't even know about that. Was this what it was like, dating a royal? Facing constant presumptions about what would come next?

His blood chilled in his veins. He was only just starting to feel again after three numb years. And he wasn't there yet. He wasn't. He couldn't offer Gabrielle anything close to marriage yet.

She held up another paper. 'Apparently there was a picture of us the day before too. My team just missed it amongst all the mine reports.'

Sullivan squinted at the paper in her hand. There was a photo of him and her walking out of the hospital. He had his arm slung around her waist, they were both dressed in scrubs and basically looking like the walking dead. He read that headline.

Who is the mystery man with Princess Gabrielle?

He shook his head and threw the broadsheet he'd been holding on the unmade bed. 'Well, I guess they found that out,' he muttered. 'Why are you so upset about this? It's nothing. It's rubbish.'

He was ignoring the wedding stuff. She couldn't speak Italian. Maybe she hadn't read that part.

Her tanned skin was pale. He could still see the slight tremor in her hands. Gabrielle started pacing around the room. 'But it's not. If people lose faith in me, Mirinez's reputation will be damaged.'

'Won't it already be damaged by the fact your brother hasn't functioned for the last few years?'

She completely ignored his comment and kept pacing. 'I still have trade agreements and business deals to finalise. This could threaten them. If other countries don't trust me to lead wisely, why should they invest in us?'

He shook his head and walked over, putting both hands on the tops of her arms. 'Stop, Gabrielle. Just stop.'

The breath she sucked in was shaky. He hated seeing her like this. But he also hated the fact his photo was slapped across the front of a newspaper. He'd always been a fairly private person and the fact it was an intensely personal moment sparked a little fire inside him. He glanced at the paper again, trying to work out who on earth had taken the photograph. From the angle it seemed to have been taken slightly from above—none of the restaurant staff could have done that.

He pushed all thoughts away and tried to keep on track. 'Who deals with publicity for you? Release a statement saying your privacy should be respected. If you have to, give them my name, rank and serial number. I suspect they already know—that just wasn't interesting enough to report. There's nothing else to find out about me, Gabrielle. I'm a surgeon. I've served in the military. I've kissed you. That's it. They can spin it whatever way they like. What you need to do is tell them about *you*.

'Arrange an interview—tell the world what you've come back to. Tell them about the work you've been doing on TB. Tell them about how the mining accident has been handled and your plans for the future to make sure it doesn't happen again. Tell them you've been working in the hospital as well as trying to catch up on work your brother left behind.' He waved his hand. 'They've painted you here as some kind of lightweight socialite, someone who can't be trusted to make decisions. This isn't you. Show them who the real you is.'

Her voice cracked. 'I can't do this. I just can't. I never wanted to do this anyway. I just want to go back to being a doctor. *Just* a doctor. I'm sorry you've been caught up in all this. It's not fair. Newspapers are awful. Some reporters will spend their lives looking for something to splash on the front page. They hound your family and friends, as if invading everyone's privacy is their given right.'

Sullivan stepped back. Something about this felt off. Something he couldn't quite put his finger on. Yes, Gabrielle was embarrassed to have been caught in a compromising position but her reaction seemed about more than that.

His insides curled up. Was she embarrassed by him? Worried that the world might read more into their relationship than she'd like? The truth was, he didn't even know what this relationship was—so how could anyone else?

Was she embarrassed by the presumption they might marry? Did she think he might never be marriage material? He'd never had to think that way before. That he might not be good enough. It was a whole new experience.

Particularly when he was trying to come to terms with the fact Gabrielle seemed to be bringing him out of the fog he'd been in for the last three years. Was this just a fling for her?

But there was something in those dark eyes that looked like intense worry. She'd been brought up in the public eye. Maybe not completely under the spotlight like some of the other European royal families, but he would have thought she might have more experience of the media than someone like him.

He took her hand. 'Get dressed. Come with me to the hospital. We have patients to review.' It seemed like the most sensible suggestion. In the hospital Gabrielle was completely at home, confident in her abilities and could focus on the job. Out here she was floundering.

Her head gave a slow nod. The hospital must have sounded like a safe place. 'Once we've reviewed all the patients we need to, we can make a plan.' He gave a little frown. 'Franz should be helping you with this. I suppose you should either release a statement or give an interview.' He took a deep breath. 'I'll support you whatever you want to do.'

A tiny part of him wanted to walk away from all this. But Gabrielle needed support. And the selfish side of him realised that even though she didn't know it, she was supporting him too.

This was the first real relationship he'd been part of since his father had died. He'd always been confident with women. But his career choices had meant he was constantly on the move. It was difficult to form meaningful relationships when you didn't know where you'd be in six months. And the truth was—he hadn't wanted to.

But now? Something was different. Gabrielle was like a breath of fresh air just when he needed it. Just a glimpse of her dark eyes brought a smile to his face. He wasn't quite as ready to walk away as he had been in the past.

She gave a nod. 'I'll meet you back here in half an hour,' she said as she disappeared out the door.

Sullivan didn't even get a chance to reply.

He stared at the crumpled broadsheet on the bed. Why did that discarded piece of paper suddenly feel like his life?

Her brain was spinning. Her initial worry about being caught without any appropriate clothes had disappeared the instant Franz had delivered the news.

She ignored everyone in the corridor as she strode towards her apartments, opening the door and walking straight through and flicking on the shower.

The reports were bad enough. Doubtless by tomorrow others would have picked up the story and started digging for more dirt.

And that was what she feared most.

People knew that Andreas had abdicated. They didn't know about the mess he'd left behind. And they didn't know the rest of it. The missing million euros she'd just found out about.

When the investigative journalists got their hands on that news it would make headlines anywhere.

And she would be left to face the music.

She couldn't share this. She couldn't tell Sullivan.

He hadn't signed up for this. He hadn't signed up for *anything*.

Her skin was still tingling. Tingling from where he'd touched her.

She stepped under the shower and let the hot water sting her skin.

Everything about Sullivan felt so right, but how could it be, when everything else in the world was so wrong?

She was trying to come to grips with the fact that this would be her life now.

Head of State.

She should have been more realistic. She should have realised this could always be a possibility. But she'd been selfish. She'd only been thinking of herself and had run away, fulfilling her dreams and ambitions to be a doctor.

She tipped her head back, allowing the water to sluice over her face, grabbing the scented shampoo and rubbing briskly.

When Sullivan had taken her to bed last night everything else had flown straight out of the window. Her worries, her fears about her changing life. She'd only concentrated on him.

Her feelings about Sullivan were so tangled up she really couldn't think straight at all. That smile. The feel of his muscles under the palms of her hands. For her—nirvana.

And outside that, he was so grounded. So matter-of-fact. He'd stepped into a crisis situation and responded without question. She liked that about him. She maybe even loved that about him.

She hadn't contemplated how much last night would mean to her. The connection she would feel with Sullivan. How right everything could feel.

But reports like the ones in the newspaper might well scare him off. *Marriage?* Neither of them could even contemplate something like that right now.

She had to concentrate all her time on her duties, on running the country. That was where her priorities should lie right now. Even if her heart didn't feel as if it wanted that.

The thing was, she felt that if Sullivan was by her side she might actually be able to do this.

When she was with him, instead of being filled with worry, she could actually remember some of the things about Mirinez she'd always loved and had just forgotten about.

The people were great. In previous years the economy and business had been thriving. The number of celebrities who stayed here because of the principality's tax-haven status was rising all the time. Mirinez was considered a glamorous place to visit and because of the celebrities the tourist industry was thriving. In light of the bad news she'd heard about the missing million euros, she probably needed to use that to Mirinez's advantage.

She flicked off the shower and grabbed her robe, wrapping it around her as she towel-dried her hair.

Would Sullivan even contemplate staying here, continuing a relationship? Part of her didn't want to even consider it. Sullivan seemed to be a workaholic. He went on one mission after another. And there was something curious about that drive. It was almost as if she had to dig a little deeper. It was obvious he was still mourning the death of his father but Sullivan was too alpha to ever admit that. Did he even realise himself?

She sighed as she sat down in front of the mirror.

All she really knew was that she didn't want him to leave. But the private hospitals of Mirinez would never keep the attention of a surgeon like Sullivan. There would need to be something else. Need to be something more.

Her heart squeezed in her chest. She'd like it if that could be her.

But what were the chances of that?

As soon as they set foot in the hospital Gabrielle started to relax a little more. She instantly moved into doctor mode. Someone asked her to check an X-ray regarding a potential case of TB and she looked so enthused he could have cheered.

His patients were doing well. He scheduled surgery for the next day for one of the burns victims, then spent a considerable amount of time talking to the miner from China and his family to assure them that he was being taken care of.

Gabrielle was at ease here. He watched her talk enthusiastically to patients, offering comfort as she reviewed their conditions and making plans for the future. Just like in Nambura, patients seemed drawn to her. Gabrielle wasn't a princess here. She balanced being the ultimate professional while showing care and attention to her patients.

Every now and then their eyes met and she gave him the kind of smile that had multiple effects, some on his body and some on his mind.

One of the nurses gave him a knowing look as she noticed him watching. 'I hadn't met Princess Gabrielle before now.' She gave a little nod of her head. 'She's great. I wish she'd stay around as a doctor. Philippe, our director, has had a total personality transplant in the last few days.'

Sullivan looked at her in surprise. 'What do you mean?'

The nurse met his gaze. 'I've been here five years. I came from France. Private hospitals here are all about money. For as long as I've known him, Philippe has been so uptight, so focused on profit and being the first place to offer the next big surgery.'

'And now?' Sullivan didn't know whether to feel irritated or intrigued. What had caused the change in the hospital director?

She sighed. 'He's better. I think because Gabrielle told him that the government and mining company would cover the medical costs he can relax a little. I think Philippe usually spends half his life chasing down accounts that haven't been paid.' She held out her hand, gesturing. 'Sixty per cent of our beds are currently filled with patients from the mining accident.'

Sullivan had never really worked in private practice. He'd gone from training to serving in the military—to working for Doctors Without Borders.

It gave him a bit of perspective about the pressures others were under—including Gabrielle. 'Money makes the world go round. I hope the mining company comes through on its promises.'

The nurse waved her hand as she moved away. 'If they don't, Gabrielle has promised the government will pick up the entire tab.' She smiled and started walking backwards as she made her way down the corridor. 'If you can, try and persuade her to keep working here sometimes.' She winked at Sullivan. 'You too, if you like. The surgeons have been talking. They're impressed.'

Sullivan couldn't help the smile that appeared on his face. Getting praise from a patient was always the best thing, but getting praise from colleagues in a competitive business like this? That was pretty good too. 'Thanks. But, hey, who says I have any influence over Gabrielle?'

The nurse tapped the side of her nose as she disappeared around the corner. 'I can see it…' she interlinked her fingers '…the connection. You two light up the place like a Christmas tree.' She winked again. 'And you could cook sausages with the sizzle in the air between you.'

She disappeared around the corner, leaving Sullivan smiling and shaking his head.

Ten hours later Gabrielle had never felt better. This felt normal. This felt real. She'd reviewed ten patients at length, changing prescriptions, altering care plans and discussing their care with them and their nurses. That was just at the first hospital. She'd then left St George's and headed to Princess Elizabeth's to review another three patients there.

Franz had caught up with her at one point. There were more legal documents to be signed, a briefing from one of the European lawyers about a contract dispute, but he didn't mention the missing money again. He looked gaunt and she was aware he knew exactly where she'd been all day. She put her hand over his. 'Let's talk about other matters tomorrow,' she'd said quietly.

'Of course,' he'd agreed. He'd pursed his lips then added, 'Are you sure about this statement?'

She'd written it by email while in St George's, given it ten minutes of her time and no more. She had patients to attend to and wasn't here to court the reporter's interest. She gave a quick nod of her head. 'Send it as it is.' She would deal with any queries tomorrow.

She wanted to do something else this evening. Something else entirely. By the time the idea had fully formed in her mind she was practically running down the corridor. She threw off one set of clothes and grabbed another. Five minutes later she knocked on Sullivan's door.

'Come in.' He was trying to decide how to persuade Gabrielle she should find a way to keep working as a doctor.

The door swung open and Gabrielle stood there, leaning against the doorjamb. She was wearing the tight jeans that drove him crazy, a grey hooded zip-up top and had a red baseball cap pulled low over her face. 'Ready?' she asked.

He spun around from the desk. 'Ready for what?'

She sauntered across the room towards him. 'To play hookey with me, of course.'

He stood up and walked over to meet her. 'You want to play hookey?'

She laid her hands on his chest. 'What I want is to go to the movies, watch the best action film on the planet and eat my body weight in popcorn.'

Now he understood the clothes. He ran his eyes up and down her body then wagged his finger. 'Oh, no. You can't do that. It's a dead giveaway.'

'What?' She looked down and then from side to side. 'What am I doing?'

He folded his arms and nodded his head. 'You're not doing it now. That's better.'

He walked over to the closet and pulled out jeans and a T-shirt. 'Got a spare baseball hat? I didn't think it would be required clothing in Mirinez.'

She wrinkled her nose. 'What was I doing? What'll get me recognised?'

He fastened his jeans and slid his feet into a kicked-in pair of baseball boots. He rummaged through his backpack and pulled out a navy blue hoodie.

'Smiling.' He winked at her. 'Put that smile away. It's recognisable anywhere.'

Her cheeks flushed a little, but the sparkle in her eyes made him pull her closer. He breathed in, filling his senses with her light floral scent as he pushed her hat back and dropped a kiss on her lips. She wrapped her hands around his neck and whispered in her ear, 'Don't distract me, or we won't get anywhere.'

'Hmm...would that be so bad?'

She touched the side of his shadowed jaw, her nail scraping along the stubble he now wished he had shaved. 'Haven't you heard? You're the delinquent doc. You're supposed to be leading me astray.'

'Oh, I can do that, no problem.'

She pulled her hat back on. 'Then get me out of here. Let's go and watch a film.'

He rolled his eyes as he slid his hand into hers. 'This is crazy. I want you to know, you're the only girl on the planet I'd do this for.' He opened the door and glanced down the corridor. It was surprisingly empty. 'I'm assuming you know a back way out of here?'

She gave him an innocent expression. 'I might. Let's just say I didn't waste all my teenage years in the palace.'

'I thought you were a good girl. The study queen.'

She put her hand on his arm. 'That's what I wanted to the world to know. The rest?' She held up her hand and gave him a wicked look.

He shook his head. He liked it that Gabrielle had a rebellious side. He also liked it that she'd obviously learned a number of years ago how to manipulate the press. Maybe it was time to refresh those skills.

They crept down the corridor, looking both ways as they went. Some of the palace and security staff were talking at the top of the one of the staircases. He put his finger to his lips. Gabrielle gestured with her head to the right. 'This way,' she whispered as they ducked down another corridor. She took them into the library, checked over her shoulder and pushed against one of the panels on the wall. After long seconds, the wooden panel slid to the side.

Sullivan couldn't help it. His mouth hung open. 'You have got to be joking.'

'What?' She smiled.

He held out his hand. 'A hidden door, a secret passage? No way.' He kept shaking his head but couldn't stop smiling.

She shrugged her shoulders. 'The palace is hundreds of years old. There are numerous plans. What you find depends on which set of plans you look at.'

'This is like something from a movie.' He stuck his head into the dark corridor and pulled it back out in wonder, squinting at the dimensions of the room they were in. The wooden panels were deceptive. He was still frowning as he walked back out into the corridor to check the overall size of the rooms.

'Stop it,' hissed Gabrielle, laughing and pulling him back inside. 'You can think about all that later. Now we need to go.'

He was still shaking his head as she led him down the twisting and turning dark corridor. *'Phwoff!'* he said, wiping the cobwebs from his face. 'I take it no one else has gone down here in years.'

She couldn't stop grinning. 'Probably not. Andreas used to sneak his girlfriends in and out this way when we were teenagers.'

He squeezed her hand. '*Just* Andreas?'

She gave him a smart glance. 'Can I pretend I'm an American and plead the fifth?'

He rolled his eyes as they turned a corner with a chink of light at the end. She pressed her hands up against the door and pushed. Nothing happened.

He put his hands next to hers. 'You'd better tell me now, are we going to end up in that place in the kids' story where they go through the back of the cupboard?'

She shook her head. 'No. Just Mirinez. But who knows? It might already feel like Narnia to you.'

'Narnia. That was it.' He pushed hard alongside her and the door creaked open slowly.

Long grass and a tall hedge were impeding the doorway. Gabrielle flattened her back and slunk along behind the hedge out into the palace gardens, Sullivan followed suit and looked around, trying to get his bearings.

'Where are we?'

'Opposite side of the palace from your apartments.'

He looked back at the hedge. The door was completely hidden. He put his hands on his hips. 'I honestly can't believe there's a door there. I also can't believe you just didn't tell Security you were going out without them.'

Gabrielle shook her head. 'Where's the fun in that?' She waved her hand. 'Anyway, do you really think Arun would let me get away with it?'

She skirted along the hedge until they reached a large security gate, which she opened with an old-fashioned brass key.

It opened out onto the road and they walked half a mile to the nearest tram stop. Gabrielle pulled her hat down. 'Hope you've got plenty of money. I eat a *lot* of popcorn.'

He patted his pocket. 'I think I can manage to keep you in popcorn.'

They settled into a seat on the tram. No one even looked at Gabrielle and Sullivan pulled his hood up. As the tram travelled through the city she pointed out different areas to Sullivan. 'This is Felixstock. It's one of the city suburbs. Houses are cheaper here and a lot of the locals stay in this area. There are a few community clinics as a lot of the residents of Mirinez don't have their own health insurance. Some get health insurance through their employers.'

'But the rest don't?'

She shook her head. 'No, it's a bit of an issue. I'd really like to do some shifts in one of the community clinics.'

Sullivan gave her a smile. It seemed that he

wasn't going to have to persuade her to continue being a doctor after all. The seed was already planted and growing. 'I think, once you get over the chaos period you'll be able to balance things to your advantage.'

He could see her biting the inside of her cheek. She let out a long slow breath. 'Here's hoping. I can't imagine reaching that point right now.' Then she wrinkled her nose. 'The chaos period?'

He nodded. 'Sorting out the disaster your brother left behind.'

There was the oddest expression on her face and he knew instantly that there was still something she wasn't telling him. Something coiled up low in his gut. He'd thought they were getting closer. Thought that she trusted him. But there were obviously some things she still didn't want to share.

What did he know about running a country? There could probably be a million things that Gabrielle could never discuss with him. He shifted in the tram seat.

As the city passed by outside he sucked in a breath. Something was eating away at his brain. Thoughts of Oregon, going back home and his father. He'd ignored another call from Gibbs. A call that would doubtless have offered a chance for the next mission—another chance to avoid going home.

He pushed those thoughts away as Gabrielle tugged at his arm and jumped up. The cinema was at the end of the street. They walked hand in hand, past the restaurant they'd eaten in the other night, and joined the queue outside the cinema.

The doors opened and they filed in. Gabrielle tried to melt into the background as he bought the tickets and the popcorn and soda. The cinema was dark when they entered and the adverts were already playing. 'Where do you want to sit?' he whispered to Gabrielle.

She winked at him. 'How about the back row?'

'Your wish is my command.' He gave a mock bow and led her up to the back row.

They settled in their seats. He slung his arm around her and she settled her head on his shoulder. Two minutes later she pulled her hat off. Her soft hair was just under his nose. The aroma of raspberries drifted up around him. As the film progressed Gabrielle tilted her head up to him. 'What do you think?'

He leaned closer. 'I think I need a distraction.' She tasted of popcorn and lemonade as her lips parted easily against his and her hand slid up around his neck. Even fully clothed he could feel her curves against him, reminding him of their night together. He slid his hand under her top, her silky skin warm beneath the palm of his hand. He sensed her smile as they kissed. 'You make me feel fifteen again,' she whispered as his hand closed over her hardened nipple. Her kissing intensified, her hips tilting towards him and one hand running along the side of his jaw. Her other hand slid over the front of his jeans.

'Is this how you behaved in the cinema at fifteen?' he growled.

'Always,' she teased, before she pulled her lips from his and settled back to watch the film.

Sullivan glanced sideways at her and adjusted his position in his seat. 'Now, that's what I call a distraction,' he said as he glanced at his watch. 'This is going to be the longest ninety minutes of my life.'

'Here, have some popcorn.' She dumped it in his lap with a cheeky glance.

The next morning the papers seemed to have changed their mind about her delinquent doc.

There was a fuzzy picture of them locked in each other's arms in the cinema. It seemed her disguise hadn't gone unnoticed. Arun gave her a stern stare as he handed over the morning's papers. '*Don't* do that again.' He narrowed his gaze and raised his eyebrows. 'I wanted to see that movie.' He strode off down the corridor.

She smiled as she settled down to check the press. Her staff knew she wasn't particularly adept at translating languages so they'd translated all the headlines pertaining to Gabrielle and Sullivan.

This time they'd actually found out a little more about Sullivan. They named his father and his great service as an admiral in the US navy. They'd found a photo of Sullivan from a few years ago. She had no idea where it had been taken—but it could have been used for an action movie. He was in uniform with a desert background. His face was smeared with dust, but he was on the ground, attending to a patient. He was clearly focused on the job.

He was pointing to something in the distance and shouting. The sleeves of his uniform were pushed high up on his arms, revealing his defined biceps. The intensity in his face seemed to emanate from every pore on his body. He hadn't noticed the photographer—or he wasn't bothering with them. He was totally in the moment.

The photo would stop just about every woman in their tracks. And if the photo didn't, the words underneath might: *Hero Doc*.

The press had certainly changed their tune.

Beneath the article was the statement she'd released via the Palace press office yesterday.

Princess Gabrielle has arrived in Mirinez to take up the role of Head of State after the abdication of Prince Andreas. She is ready and willing to take up this position, serving the people of Mirinez to the best of her ability.

Princess Gabrielle makes no excuses for the fact that she is a doctor. Her experience served her well following the recent mine explosion, and she will continue to serve as a doctor, in a community setting, as well as carrying out her state duties.

Princess Gabrielle was accompanied on her return home by Dr Sullivan Darcy, a surgeon who has worked for Doctors Without Borders and served in the US military. His skills proved vital in dealing with the victims of burns from the mining explosion and Princess Gabrielle is grateful to have his expertise at this time.

Everything would be almost perfect if it wasn't for the slightly grainy picture underneath of the two of them locked in each other's arms. It made it look as if she were trying to keep him a secret. As if she was ashamed.

The hardest part of the statement had been the part about Sullivan. What should she call him? A friend? A boyfriend? A colleague?

In the end she'd taken the easiest way out and not called him anything. Just using the words that he'd 'accompanied' her.

She was so torn. Her heart was going one place and her head another.

She looked at the list of responsibilities that she still needed to tackle as Head of State. As time progressed it was gradually reducing. There were still a number of critical issues to be dealt with—not least the one about the missing money. There were also a number of duties she still had to fulfil.

Duties were always the things she'd hated most as a child. Being forced to dress up and behave at certain state events had never been her favourite way to spend time. But now her childhood days and teenage rebellion years had long since passed, she could look on them with adult eyes.

Tomorrow night there was a state banquet. It had been arranged when Andreas had still been head of state. With everything else that was going on, she hadn't even given it a moment's thought.

As she looked at the guest list now, she could see the names of dignitaries, members of other royal families and members of parliament. Several of the people on the guest list were also featured on her list of responsibilities as Head of State. Talking in person was always so much better than talking on the phone. There were a few essential conversations she could have that evening to mend bridges or smooth over troubled waters that her brother had created.

She licked her dry lips.

Maybe this was a good way to hint at something else. To the press. To the people of Mirinez. And to the members of staff in the palace. If she invited Sullivan to the event as her partner—officially—that would send a message.

Her heart fluttered in her chest. Was this the right thing to do?

She walked over to her closet and pulled open the doors, running her eyes over the clothes. It had been such a long time since she'd been to anything officially 'royal' that she really didn't have much suitable. Franz had arranged for a few suits and work clothes to be available to her as soon as she'd arrived.

A banquet was something else entirely. And Gabrielle didn't spend hours deciding what to wear. As long as it was suitable, covered everything it should, and felt good, she would be happy. She'd never been the type of girl that was a clothes horse. She picked up the phone. 'Franz, I'll need something to wear for the state banquet—can you arrange that? And can you let people know that Dr Darcy will be my guest and find something suitable for him too? Thanks.'

She put down the phone and gave a nervous smile.

Finally, she had something to look forward to.

* * *

The surgery had taken longer than expected. His back ached. It had been a long time since that had happened. In Helmand Provence he'd frequently been on his feet in surgery for sixteen hours at a time. But it was odd. The heat of the environment that normally caused so many other issues had seemed to relieve any muscular aches and pains.

He strode down the corridor towards his apartments. The surgery seemed to have been successful. He'd had to graft a large piece of skin onto the hand, ensuring there was enough elasticity to allow adequate movement and dexterity for the fingers. Hand surgery was one of the trickiest, particularly around burns. But he'd review how things looked in the morning to ensure the best outcome for his patient. Surgery was only the first step. This miner would have months of physical therapy ahead. It would be a long, hard road.

It was unusual. The palace seemed busier than normal. More staff. More cars in the courtyard. There was a buzz in the air.

He opened the door to his apartments and stopped. A few suits were hanging from the outside of the wardrobe, along with a variety of shirts and ties, a military dress uniform and a variety of shoes.

Was he going somewhere?

Mikel, the security guard, appeared at his shoulder. 'Dr Darcy, I was looking for you.'

'What's up, Mikel? Why has my room turned into a department store?'

Mikel smiled. 'There's a state banquet tonight. It had already been arranged before you and Princess Gabrielle arrived—it will be the first that she's officially hosted.' Mikel pointed to the clothes. 'Anyway, you are the Princess's guest. Arun arranged for a few choices of clothes for you.' He gestured towards the uniform. 'He wasn't sure what you would want to wear.' He gave a cheeky grin. 'And don't worry. This time everything will fit perfectly.'

Mikel turned and headed for the door. 'Banquet starts at seven. You'll be expected at Princess Gabrielle's apartments at six-thirty.'

He disappeared out the door and Sullivan sank into the armchair next to the window. He was exhausted. What he'd really like to do was lie on top of the bed and search TV channels for a baseball game—the one thing he actually did miss while away on all his missions.

There was a tray on the table next to him. With a pot of coffee and…he lifted the silver dome… his favourite sandwich, a Philly steak cheese. He shook his head as the smell drifted around him. The palace staff were completely obliging and had obviously read his mind. He poured the coffee and tore into the sandwich as he looked at the suits hanging outside the wardrobe. He didn't even want to think about how much they had cost.

His eyes flicked to the dress uniform. He moved over and fingered the gold braid on the navy jacket. The cap was sitting on top of the nearby table. Would he be comfortable wearing his dress uniform? He had an honourable discharge from the US Army. If he had permission, he could still wear his dress uniform. The question was—did he want to?

While his time in the military had been an intense but enjoyable experience, just looking at the uniform reminded him of his father. He had numerous photographs of his father in his own dress uniform. As his father's whole career had been in the military, his uniform had almost been like his second skin.

He dropped his hand and moved over to the nearest suit. The first touch of the fabric told him its quality. He pressed his lips together. He didn't need to deal with the other stuff tonight.

It was eating away at him. Things only seemed to be intensifying as his relationship with Gabrielle blossomed. They were always there, always burning away at his soul—probably creating an ulcer in his stomach—always letting him know that he had unfinished business. The wall he had created around himself was starting to be eaten away by little chinks. Chinks he still didn't know if he could accommodate. One of the black suits would be fine. He walked into the bathroom and flicked the handle on the shower.

What was a state banquet anyway?

She opened the door as soon as he knocked. 'Wow, so that's what you look like when you actually wear the jacket as well as the shirt and trousers.'

He smiled. 'Hey.' He looked down. 'This is actually a different pair of trousers and a different shirt from the other night. I did contemplate the jeans from the cinema.'

She gave him a gentle shove. 'Don't go there.' She stepped forward and pretended to straighten his tie. Anything to get up close and personal.

His hand went straight to her hip. She could feel the heat from his palm instantly through the fine satin of her dress. He rubbed his palm gently up and down the curve of her hip and waist.

'If this is what we wear to state banquets then I'm all in.'

She gave a little groan. 'Behave.' She'd picked a demurely styled navy blue satin dress. The bodice was also covered in lace and scattered with sequins that showed the tanned skin on her shoulders and around the top of neckline hint through the lace. In her ears she had large diamond and sapphire earrings and her hair was pinned up.

'How can I behave when you look like this?' he whispered.

She was wearing heavier make-up than normal, a little glitter enhancing her dark eyes and a brighter red lipstick. She licked her lips as she glanced at him. 'You'll have to behave. Haven't you heard? You're my official date. One day a delinquent doc, the next day the hero doc.' She stood on tiptoe and whispered in his ear, 'Who knows what tomorrow will bring?'

'Am I allowed to use my imagination?' The brush of her hair, the feel of her soft skin against his was enough to send his senses racing. He wasn't sure at all what tonight would entail, but he was happy to be by her side.

Gabrielle was nervous. This was a big night for her. It was a big night for them. And she still really hadn't taken the chance to sit down and explain things to Sullivan.

Part of her wondered what he might say. Telling him that this invitation might mean…that she was telling the world she hoped he'd stay around seemed desperate. And she had never been desperate.

But then again, she'd never been Head of State of Mirinez before. And as much as she hated it, any minute now the press would move on to the next stage. This time next week they would decide that, yes, Gabrielle would be marrying Sullivan and start contemplating a date...then speculating about a family.

She wanted to be back in Paris with Sullivan, spending long lazy days and even longer nights in bed, just waiting for a call for the next mission.

Chances were, at this point she would still be nervous. They would always need to have that 'conversation'. The one where they decided if their fling was over, or if it meant something more.

Truth was, she was falling a little in love with Sullivan. He made her feel safe. One look from him, one hint of twinkle in his eye and it felt as if a thousand tiny caterpillars were marching over her skin. Just the upward curl of his smile meant her blood would start to race around her body. As for the feel of his lips connecting with hers...

She didn't want to lose that feeling. She wanted to grab it and hold on with both hands.

But Sullivan seemed to have spent the last few years on a never-ending mission. She couldn't expect him to give all that up. She would never ask him to. But would he consider something else? Would he consider somewhere and someone to come home to?

She tilted her chin up to his and wrapped

her arms around his neck. He met her lips eagerly. This felt like coming home. His lips parted against hers, his tongue running along the edges. It was easy to welcome his kiss. She inhaled his fresh scent. Probably pure pheromones. The guy had them by the bagload.

He eventually pulled back and rested his forehead against hers while she caught her breath. He smiled and lifted his thumb to her lips. 'Might have smudged your lipstick. Can't have you leaving here looking anything less than perfect.'

She lifted her fingers to his lips too. 'I might have left you with my mark.' She rubbed the remnants of her red lipstick from his face.

He gave her a crooked kind of smile. There was something in his eyes. Not the twinkle that she was used to—this time it was thoughtful sincerity. It almost took her breath away. 'I could get used to that.'

She stepped back. Should she speak to him now? Should she ask him how he felt about the future—the possibility of a future with her?

There was a knock at the door. Franz entered and gave her an approving smile. 'Perfect, you're ready, Princess Gabrielle. A large number of our guests have already arrived and are being entertained. I think it's time to join them. Are you ready?'

He looked between her and Sullivan. She

couldn't help but notice that Sullivan almost got an approving glance too.

She quickly fixed her lipstick then slid her arm into Sullivan's, giving him a smile as her stomach did a few somersaults. 'Yes, we're ready, aren't we?'

He nodded in agreement as they headed out of the apartments. As they reached the stairs she could hear the noise from beneath them. The ballroom was buzzing. A string quartet was playing in the corner and palace staff was circulating with silver trays containing glasses of champagne and hors d'oeuvres.

She gave Sullivan's arm a little squeeze as they descended the stairs. This would be his first experience of what royal life could entail. She crossed her fingers, silently praying that everything would go well and he wouldn't be on the first plane out of here.

But everything went like a charm. Sullivan moved easily around the room. He was a seasoned professional and his language skills took everyone by surprise. He was also a fabulous advocate for Doctors Without Borders, engaging delegates from other countries in conversations about working across the globe and the type of health interventions needed.

She was trying her best too, working her way through a number of difficult conversations that were clearly overdue. In the end, the paths seemed smoother.

The royal dining room was set up in shades of gold and cream. As always, the staff had done an immaculate job. Franz had seated people carefully—always a challenge at a state dinner. But the wine flowed and the food was served quickly.

Sullivan was across the table and further down from her. She could see him talking to the people on either side of him, neither of whom she could place. But from time to time his eyes drifted off. Her heart gave a squeeze when the expression on his face was almost pained. But as soon as someone next to him started talking again, he smiled and gave them his full attention.

If she didn't know better she'd think he was feeling uncomfortable. But she'd seen that look on Sullivan's face before. It was always fleeting. Always almost hidden.

She'd been so busy thinking about herself and her country, so busy hoping that Sullivan would feel the same way she did and want to continue their relationship, that she hadn't even stopped to wonder about those moments.

Relationships should be a partnership. He was supporting her. But was she supporting him in return?

She shifted uncomfortably in her chair, the sequins on her dress digging in a little around her arm. The chancellor of a neighbouring country brushed her arm to start another conversation and she responded. But Sullivan was still at the forefront of her mind.

Why did she feel like a teenager again, instead of a Princess?

Dinner had been fine. The guests and company had been interesting. He'd had a number of conversations about health issues that Doctors Without Borders supported. He also had avenues to explore in future months.

But the table had been huge, filled at either side and accommodating more than three hundred people. It was impossible to know everyone who was there.

He'd watched Gabrielle. She was the perfect hostess. Beautiful, considerate, genuine and very, very measured.

It was almost amusing. If they'd been on a mission he was sure she would have told a few diplomats exactly what she thought of them, but the role of Head of State was vastly different from managing a team in the jungle.

But he'd watched the rest of the people around the table. As the night progressed he could see Gabrielle moving up in their estimations. For some strange reason it made his heart swell with pride.

Everything about her—her smile, the toss of her hair, her laugh—seemed to connect with him in a way that was deeper than anything he'd ever experienced before.

He should be singing. He should be shouting from the rooftops and he wanted to, he really did.

But something was holding him back.

For the first time in his life he really wanted to make a commitment. He wanted to sit down and have that 'what if' conversation. The one where he could tell her just how he felt and see how he could make things work.

For a few days he just wished the whole royal scenario hadn't happened. But this was Gabrielle's birthright. She had responsibilities and if he loved her the way he thought he might, then he had to accept that.

He knew that she was struggling. And he wanted to help. He did.

So why did he feel as if there was a rope around his waist, pulling him back? Stopping him from going where he wanted to be.

The truth was that he had personal issues to deal with first. He'd left part himself back in the house in Oregon three years ago when he'd buried his dad.

Grief was a strange and curious thing. It started as an overwhelming sensation that the world sympathised with for a few weeks.

Then it was expected to gradually disperse.

In all honesty, he'd expected it to disperse too. But it hadn't.

Instead, it had stayed. And grown. Starting as a little seed, it had changed to a sprouting plant and turned into a vine that had crept up and wound its way around his heart and soul, telling him to deal with it as the blackness had clouded in the background.

He was a doctor. A medic. He'd seen things on his tours of duty that would haunt him for ever. But he'd accepted that part of his life. He was supposed to be tough. A delinquent even. A hero.

Those words actually sent a chill down his spine.

But most of all he was a man. Add all those things together—doctor, man, delinquent, hero— and he should be easily equipped to deal with the loss of his father.

His way of dealing with it was constantly being busy, of constantly having his mind and body focusing on something else.

If he really wanted to move forward and work out a way to continue this relationship with Gabrielle then he had to find a way to put the past behind him.

It was the voice he recognised first. His head turned automatically to try and locate the source. Then it was the figure. The broad shoulders and familiar dress uniform. The last time he'd seen Admiral Sands had been at his father's funeral.

At the same time Joe Sands looked over and caught Sullivan's eye. The recognition took less than a few seconds before he lifted his hand, waved and started to walk in Sullivan's direction.

A tightness spread across Sullivan's chest, his mouth instantly dry. There was a buzzing in his ears, as if he'd just been surrounded by a swarm of angry wasps. Joe Sands looked as relaxed as always. Time had been kind to him. Sullivan knew he must be in his late seventies; he'd retired twenty years ago. He'd been one of first people to get in touch following the death of his father, and he'd made a few attempts since then to keep in contact with Sullivan.

He slapped Sullivan's arm. 'Sullivan Darcy. It's good to see you. How have you been?'

Sullivan gave the briefest of nods as his mouth tried to formulate a reply. Even though he'd had a dress uniform in his apartments and had chosen not wear it, seeing someone else dressed that way had caught him unawares. He hadn't expected it—not here, in Mirinez. He'd got out of the way of being in the company of men in US uniforms. His father had been buried in his dress uniform— as many military men were—and as the light glinted from Joe Sands's buttons the hairs on the back of Sullivan's neck stood on end.

He finally found some words. 'I'm good. Still working.'

Joe was as amiable as ever. 'I never expected to see you here in Mirinez. And you're with Gabrielle? That's wonderful. She's a beauty. Smart too. Your father would be so proud.'

Would he? It was the oddest feeling. Sullivan suddenly felt very young. He'd always wanted his father's approval. He'd always had it.

But in the last three years parts of his life had played on his mind. He'd been as rebellious as the usual teenager and young man—there were a few things his father had found about, a lot he hadn't.

But he'd never really done anything serious. He'd respected his father and their relationship too much for that.

Now every decision he made came under his night-time scrutiny of whether his father would have approved or not. Sleep had deserted him.

Gabrielle had proved the best distraction yet. There was nothing like the feel of soft smooth skin to chase away any other jumbled thoughts. But when she fell asleep first, her soft steady breathing filling the air, then the crazy thoughts would find their way back in.

Part of him knew what this was. He'd been a doctor long enough to spot the signs in other people so he'd be a fool if he couldn't recognise them in himself.

But a man wasn't supposed to be unable to deal with grief. A doctor even less so.

Life had moved on. He should have too. If a therapist had asked him a question, he couldn't even give an obvious answer. No, he didn't have unresolved issues with his father. No, there had never been any real conflict. Their relationship had been strong, cemented in the fact they'd only had each other.

And since his father had died, Sullivan had felt as if he'd lost his right-hand man. In a way he had. The effects of being an adult, real-life orphan had never occurred to him.

Perhaps it was much simpler than all that. He missed him. He missed his dad every day. So many times he'd gone to pick up a phone or write an email and stopped instantly, body washed with cold at remembering his father wasn't there. It was ridiculous.

Packing up the house felt final. It was like ripping away the last part of his father that still existed.

He couldn't talk about this to anyone. They would think it pathetic. Men weren't supposed to grieve like this. Men were supposed to get to work. And he had done exactly that—for three years—because work had been the only place he'd felt safe.

And seeing Joe Sands was bringing everything back. Any minute now he'd start regaling Sullivan with stories. Stories about the visit to NASA or Washington. Stories about arguments with generals. Joe Sands had worked alongside his father for the best part of eight years. He knew things that Sullivan didn't. And part of that made him angry. He hated the fact there were memories of his father that he didn't have.

He pasted a smile onto his face and he reached out to shake Joe's hand. 'It's a real pleasure to see you again, Admiral Sands. I'd love to talk but I'm actually on duty. I helped with the mining accident in Mirinez and I've just been contacted to go and check on a patient. If we're lucky, we might be able to catch up later.'

It was all lies. And he only felt the tiniest hint of regret as he saw the wave of disappointment on Joe's face.

'You've had a call?' Gabrielle's voice cut through his thoughts. He hadn't realised she'd appeared and certainly not that she'd overheard him.

She caught sight of his face and nodded smoothly, sliding her arm into his. 'That's why I came to find you. I've had a call too.' She nodded her head. 'Good evening, Admiral. It's so nice to see you. I'm sorry we haven't had a chance to talk. Possibly tomorrow?'

The Admiral didn't seem to notice Gabrielle's

cover-up, but Sullivan's insides felt as if they were curling up and dying.

The Admiral nodded. 'It would be my pleasure.'

Gabrielle steered Sullivan towards the open doors out to the palace gardens. Her footsteps were firm. She gave a few people gracious nods as they passed but didn't stop to talk. It was clear she was on a mission.

As soon as the colder night air hit him his breath caught in his throat. It was the oddest sensation. Like breathing in, without being able to breathe back out. He'd never felt anything like it.

Gabrielle lengthened her strides as they reached the gardens. They passed the fountain and moved away from the paved pathways and across the manicured lawn.

His heart was thudding against his chest, beads of sweat breaking out on his brow. He tugged at the tie he was wearing and struggled to loosen his collar. His skin was itching.

Was he having an allergic reaction to something? What had he eaten? That was all he could liken the sensations to.

Gabrielle led him through some trees and out towards a glass and metal-framed summerhouse. Her footsteps didn't slow until they were inside and she pushed him down onto the bench seat that ran along the inside of the summerhouse.

She knelt down in front of him and unfastened the next few buttons on his shirt. 'Calm down, Sullivan. Breathe. Slow it down.'

He pulled at his collar. 'S-something's... wrong.'

She locked her dark eyes on his, her fingers pressing on the pulse at his wrist.

'Sullivan, you're breathing too quickly. You need to slow it down. We're going to do this together.'

Sweat was trickling down his back between his shoulder blades. He shrugged off his jacket, desperate to get some air around him.

Gabrielle kept talking. Calmly. Slowly.

'I'm... I'm...'

She touched his hand gently. 'You're having a panic attack, Sullivan. That's why I've not called an ambulance or taken you anywhere else.' She held up her hands. 'It's just you and me. There's no one else around. No one else noticed anything.'

Her hand rubbed up and down his. 'Breathe in for two, and out for two. Come on, you can do this.'

His head was spinning. Was she crazy? He'd never had a panic attack in his life. But things around him felt fuzzy and he could feel his heart thudding against his chest. Pain was starting to cross his ribs. Any minute now he might throw up. Could this really be a panic attack?

Her voice got firmer. Still calm, but with a little more authority. 'Work with me, Sullivan. Come on. Breathe in for two and out for two. In for two, out for two. Do it with me. You can do this.'

She was persistent. She kept talking. Softly. Steadily. Until she started to sound as if she was making sense.

He sucked in a breath to the sound of her voice.

'That's it. Do it. Follow me. In for two, out for two.'

He started following her lead. Within a few seconds she changed. 'Okay, now in for four, out for four.'

His heart was slowing. He could feel it. And the pain in his chest was easing ever so slightly. She kept talking, looking up at him with those big brown eyes laced with concern.

His skin prickled as the perspiration on his skin mixed with the cold air. His shirt was open to his waist. He'd practically stripped.

Reality started to take a grip on his brain. He'd never had an experience like that before.

He sucked in a deeper breath and ran his fingers through his now-damp hair.

He was exhausted.

He was embarrassed.

He was confused.

In the dim light, Gabrielle's dark eyes were fixed on his. He could practically see the wheels spinning in her head.

She rocked on her heels as she watched him. Now she could see that he'd calmed down she was obviously contemplating what to do next.

This was a disaster. Not just for him, but for her too. She was Head of State, this was her first official royal banquet. She should be in the palace, attending to her guests—not out here with a man who was falling to pieces.

After a few minutes of silence she stood up and sat next to him on the bench. She rubbed her hands against her thighs. It was almost like she could read his mind. Like she knew he was already concocting a hundred reasons to explain what had just happened.

She took a deep breath and slid her hand over his, intertwining their fingers together. 'What do you need?' was all she said.

It threw him. He'd been expecting a whole wave of questions.

He looked up and out through the glass into the dark night. The gardens were peaceful, immaculate. If he hadn't known the palace was just through the trees behind him, he could have sworn they were somewhere entirely private.

He said the first thing that came into his head. 'I don't know.'

Gabrielle pressed her lips together and nodded. She turned sideways on so she could face him and placed her hand on his chest. 'From the moment I met you I've admired your physique, your muscles. But now I realise that the six-pack comes at a price. You're too lean, Sullivan. And I know you don't sleep well. You think I haven't noticed, but you get up and pace around at night. Sleep is the one thing our body really needs. We need it to recharge. We need it to refresh ourselves. How long has this been going on?'

He swallowed, his mouth drier than he'd ever known it. She was leading him down a path, one he'd spent the last three years avoiding. Maybe not all the three years. But the symptoms had started pretty soon after his father's funeral. They peaked and troughed. Just like now. Whenever he actually tried to focus some thoughts about what actually might be wrong, the symptoms intensified. Just as they did whenever he was due leave and might actually have to go home. Taking a call from Gibbs was always a relief.

It was almost like getting a licence for a few hours' sleep again.

'I can say it out loud if you can't.' There was definite sadness in her voice.

He'd disappointed her. Her hero doc wasn't a hero at all.

He was just a guy who couldn't hold it together.

She touched his cheek and shook her head. 'But I don't know if that will help.' She lowered her gaze. 'It was the Admiral, wasn't it? It was seeing him. If I'd known that you knew him...' Her voice tailed off.

'You wouldn't have invited him?' The words came out much angrier than he'd intended.

She jerked and looked back at him. 'I would have warned you,' she said softly.

He cringed and closed his eyes. She might as well take a huge banner saying *Sullivan is depressed* and hang it from the palace.

He stood up and fastened the buttons on his shirt, grabbing his jacket and shrugging it back on. 'I need some space.'

She stood up next to him and nodded, her expression hurt. He didn't mean to be blunt but he couldn't help it. There was no way he could go back into that room full of people. It didn't matter that they had no clue what had just happened.

He knew.

Gabrielle knew.

That was more than enough people already.

Gabrielle picked up her skirt and took a few steps towards the entrance of the summerhouse. She turned back to look at him and licked her lips. 'I'm here for you, Sullivan. I care.' It was almost a whisper. Then she turned on her heel and disappeared through the trees.

Sullivan sagged backwards against the glass. How could she care? How could she care about a man who wasn't really a man?

It didn't matter that he was a doctor. It didn't matter that he knew the fundamentals of depression. He'd recognised grief, depression, anxiety and PTSD in a number of his colleagues in Afghanistan.

He just couldn't apply the same principles to himself.

This shouldn't happen to him. This shouldn't be his life.

But even as the thoughts crowded his head he knew how ridiculous they were. Depression could strike anyone, at any point, at any age, under any set of circumstances.

Gabrielle had vanished through the trees. His heart twisted in his chest.

He loved her. He wanted to love her.

But in order to do that fully, he had to deal with his own issues. He had to face up to the fact he wasn't infallible. He wasn't unbreakable.

Otherwise he could let the best thing that had ever happened to him slip through his fingers.

CHAPTER TEN

BEING A PRINCESS SUCKED.

Gabrielle didn't want to be in a room smiling vacantly at visiting dignitaries and listening politely to their conversation. She wanted to be with the person who needed her right now.

The pain in his eyes had felt as if it had ripped her heart out of her chest. His struggle to accept he wasn't perfect. He wasn't the person who could do and be everything.

She didn't want that for Sullivan. She'd never gone looking for a hero.

But Sullivan was too proud. He needed time. He needed space. She couldn't be his doctor. She just had to be his friend.

And that was hard. She was used to fixing people.

But this wasn't something she could fix. She couldn't stick a plaster on his grief and magic it away.

He had to find that path himself. She only hoped he would let her walk it with him.

Sleep was becoming the invincible soldier. Too far from his grasp to really get hold of. When

Arun knocked on his door after the break of day it was a welcome relief.

If he'd heard anything about last night he didn't show it. 'Dr Darcy, I just wondered what your plans were for the day.'

Sullivan rubbed the sleep from his eyes. He'd glanced in the mirror when he'd splashed water on his face earlier and knew they were bloodshot, ringed with black circles. He looked as if he'd gone ten rounds with a champion boxer.

The trouble was, his body felt as if he'd done ten rounds too. 'I just planned on going to the hospital to review my patients. Nothing else. Did you have something else in mind?'

His answer came out automatically. He was a doctor. Of course he would go and review his patients. But was that really what he should be doing?

His mind had been haunted half the night with the sad expression on Gabrielle's face as she'd walked away. She'd said she cared. Cared. It was a cryptic word.

He could have told her that he wanted to be free to love her. He could have told her that he *did* love her. But he didn't want to go into this relationship damaged. He wanted to feel as if he could commit to Gabrielle. She deserved that. She deserved to have someone by her side who could support her in everything she did. Was he capable of that right now?

Last night, he'd had his first-ever panic attack when he'd came across someone in his father's old dress uniform. It was clear he had a long way to go. Even if he was only admitting that now.

Arun was leaning against the doorjamb, giving him a cheeky kind of grin. 'We chatted about the free clinics before in Mirinez. How would you feel about giving a helping hand today?'

His stomach did a kind of flip. He could find Gabrielle. They could talk about last night. He could sit for a few hours and re-evaluate his life. His plan. He could book a ticket home and spend some time—some real time—at the house he'd been avoiding. He could find another doctor—or a counsellor—to give him steps to help him deal with his grief.

Old habits were hard to break.

Work was always a welcome distraction. He gave Arun a nod of his head, reached for a T-shirt and pulled it over his head. 'Let me brush my teeth and I'm all yours.'

She couldn't interfere. She couldn't.

But every single cell in her body wanted to interfere in every way possible.

She knew people. People who could help Sullivan if he'd let them.

She wanted to take him by the hand and lead him to that first appointment. Or be the person who sat down next to him while he just talked. She wanted to look at Sullivan's face and not notice the dark circles under his eyes and know that he'd barely slept any of the night before.

She'd walked along to his apartments earlier and found the door wide open and the place empty. For a few seconds panic had descended. He'd left. He'd walked out.

It didn't matter that she knew she could never keep him here. The thought of Sullivan leaving without a word hurt more than she could comprehend.

She'd rushed into the rooms, glimpsed the rumpled unmade bed, a drawer hanging open, and felt as if a cold wind had just rushed over her skin. But his toiletries were still in the bathroom, his backpack still in the cupboard next to his kicked-in baseball boots. Relief washed over her. He was still here—somewhere.

She made a few casual enquiries via the security staff and found out Sullivan had gone somewhere with Arun.

St George's was quiet. The staff here were ruthlessly efficient. All the patients from the mining accident were well taken care of. Some were ready to be discharged. Her reviews took less than hour. In truth, these patients could be handed over to the care of the other doctors now, but she was enjoying her time here. She was trying to fathom out a way whereby she could keep working as a doctor, as well as function as Head of State.

Every day the list of urgent things to do seemed to diminish just a little. Several of the key issues had been resolved solely by hosting the state banquet and talking to colleagues face to face. Which meant that ultimately she would have time to take a breath and decide how to manage her life.

One of the nurses gave her a wave. 'There's a call for you, Princess Gabrielle. Do you want to take it here?'

She nodded and reached over for the phone, then paused, unsure what title she should use. She shook her head then went with her instincts. 'This is Dr Cartier, what can I do for you?'

Sullivan's voice washed over her like a warming balm. 'Gabrielle. I think you might need to come down to one of the community clinics. I'm almost certain I've got a case of TB for you.'

'You're working?' She couldn't hide the surprise in her voice and cringed as soon as the words came out loudly.

'Of course I'm working. What else would I be doing?'

She winced. She could almost see the expression on his face as he said those words. 'Nothing. Of course. Which clinic are you in?'

She scribbled down a few notes about the patient. 'I can be there soon. Arrange for an X-ray in the meantime and I'll be there soon.'

'There's another thing. I've got two children who'll need some attention. One boy has symptoms of appendicitis. He needs scans and probably surgery today. And there's another with a previously undiagnosed cleft palate. He's almost four and has problems with eating and with his speech. It's not an emergency but this should have been picked up at birth. The family have no insurance. I'm not leaving a child like this.'

She could hear the frustration in his voice and instantly sympathised. She took a second, remembering where the clinic was situated, compared to the nearest hospital with facilities for children. 'Okay, tell Arun the kids will be going to St Ignatius's. I'll phone and make the arrangements. How sick is your first little boy? Do you need an ambulance to transfer him?'

She could hear a conversation going on between Sullivan and Arun.

Something inside her recoiled. That inbuilt ethic—a doctor instantly putting his patients first and treating them. She would never expect anything else from Sullivan.

But she was also aiding Sullivan's avoidance.

If she'd known he was going to work at the community clinic this morning she could have offered to go in his place. But then he would probably have been offended.

She just didn't know what to do. She just wasn't sure how to help. If she pushed him towards therapy or medication he might walk away. He might think she was interfering. And she would be.

Was that allowed?

All she knew was that she didn't want to see Sullivan suffer any more. But how did she help all that if she couldn't interfere—just a little?

She grabbed her coat and bag, signalling to Mikel that she wanted to leave. The Corborre clinic was only ten minutes from here. But as soon as she reached the car, a call came through from Franz.

'Princess Gabrielle, you're needed at the palace urgently.'

She sat forward in her seat. 'What's wrong? Something else at the mine?'

Franz hesitated. 'No. We've made some further…discoveries.'

'Discoveries?'

She had no idea where this was heading.

'About Prince Andreas.'

Her stomach rolled over. 'Has something happened to him? Is he all right? Do you know where he is?'

She heard Franz sigh. 'No. We still haven't tracked him down. We have heard some rumours he's in Bermuda.'

'Bermuda?' Why would he go there? 'So what's wrong, then?'

'It might be better to discuss that in person.'

Gabrielle felt her heart sink. She could only imagine what would come next. 'Actually, Franz, I'm on my way to see a patient at the Corborre clinic. Whatever it is that Andreas has done, just tell me.'

In her head she could hear the drum roll. Franz finally spoke. 'It seems that the one million euros wasn't entirely accurate. We've found another account with diverted funds. To a bank—'

'In Bermuda,' she finished. She leaned forward and put her head in her hands. Franz hadn't continued and the silence was ominous.

'What else?'

'We think there are a number of items missing from the palace.'

She wrinkled her brow. 'What do you mean?'

Franz cleared his throat. 'There's another safe—one that Prince Andreas used privately.'

Gabrielle nodded. 'Yes, it's in the study in my apartments. I haven't even looked at it. Was something in there?'

'The Moroccan diamond and the Plantagenet emerald.'

'What?' Beside her, Mikel jumped at the shrillness of her voice.

'But they're family heirlooms.' The Moroccan diamond was over thirty-five carats and the emerald over forty carats. They'd been part of the family collection for hundreds of years and had moved between royal sceptres and crowns.

'We think there might also be a missing painting and…some other items.'

She leaned back and put her hand on her forehead. She could only imagine what the missing items might be. The palace was full of gorgeous pieces that had been received over the last few hundred years. Fabergé eggs, Ming vases, medieval tapestries, Egyptian artefacts and even some of Henry VIII's armour.

'I want an inventory started immediately,' she said. 'And I want advice from the palace lawyers. This can't be kept secret for long. If I have to issue a warrant for my brother's arrest, I will.'

There seemed to be a stunned silence at the end of the phone. Gabrielle closed her eyes and shook her head. 'We'll talk later. I have patients to see.'

She finished the call.

She would give anything right now to be back in Narumba with Sullivan. Before she'd known she had to be Head of State. Before he'd known she was a princess. And before she'd known that the man she loved was crippled by grief.

It was selfish. She knew that. And the instant the thought appeared she pushed it aside. Things were just overwhelming her.

The brother she'd loved and grown up with had betrayed her and their country for purely selfish motives. She still couldn't quite believe it.

No wonder she'd spent the last three years in a totally different world. One where patients were the central focus, instead of the welfare of a whole country. She'd never wanted that life back more than she did at this moment.

She watched as the city streets flashed by her window. In an ideal world she'd tell Sullivan exactly what her brother had done. But he already had enough to deal with. He didn't need her problems too.

The transfer of the children went relatively smoothly. Sullivan was greeted by yet another hospital administrator who re-checked his credentials more times than entirely necessary and made him sign what felt like a billion forms.

Appendicitis was quickly confirmed with one of the boys and Sullivan scrubbed in with one of the hospital's regular surgeons to perform the surgery. The other little boy had some tests ordered and a review by an ENT specialist, who scheduled him for surgery the following day.

Sullivan waited until the little boy with appendicitis was in Recovery and had woken up before he left.

He waved off Arun as he offered to take him back to the palace. 'I'm going to go back to the clinic. Let me walk. It will do me good and I'll see some of the city.'

Arun gave him a careful nod and disappeared.

Night was just starting to fall in Chabonnex. The streets were bathed in a mixture of orange lights and purple hues from the sky. People were moving around. It was easy to spot the tourists. Cameras and phones were permanently in their hands and most of them were talking loudly.

St Ignatius's was on the outskirts of the city centre. There were still some buildings of interest nearby, but as he moved along the street it was clear he was moving towards a less affluent area of the capital.

The buildings were just a little shabbier, houses more crammed together. Restaurants were fewer and the cars parked on the street were changing from ridiculously expensive to something that the average man might be able to afford.

His phone rang as he approached the clinic. He hadn't thought to check what the hours of the clinic were but as the lights gleamed in the distance it was clear that people were still inside.

He glanced at the screen as he pulled the phone from his pocket.

Gibbs.

His breath caught in his throat.

His finger paused over the green light. It would be so easy to push the phone back in his pocket and ignore the call.

It would be even easier to answer and just automatically say yes to the next mission. That's what he'd always done before.

After his panic attack last night he'd more or less left himself open to scrutiny by Gabrielle. She would ask. She would pry. She would try to fix him.

In a way it was ironic. He'd come to Mirinez to support her. To help her in a difficult situation. He didn't like it when things were reversed.

He could jump on a plane right now and be in another country in a matter of hours. Forget about all of this. Pretend it had never happened.

His footsteps slowed as he pressed answer and put the phone to his ear. 'Gibbs, it's Sullivan. What is it this time?'

'Sullivan, it's great to get you. Listen, I know you're just back but I'm a man short for a specialist mission in Syria. We need an experienced surgeon and your language skills would be a huge bonus.'

Sullivan could feel an uncomfortable prickle on his skin, like a million little insects crawling all over him. His tongue was stuck to the roof of his mouth, his mind spinning.

Yes, yes, of course I'll go. It's just one more mission. I'm needed. I can make a difference.

A bead of sweat ran down his brow. He wiped it away angrily.

I can sort this other stuff out later. I'll take a proper break after the next mission. I'll take some time away then. I've lasted this long.

'So you would leave probably some time in the next twenty-four hours. No need to ask where you are. I've seen you in the press. Such a shame about Gabrielle. We hate to lose her. She's one of the best doctors we've got for TB. I'll need to find about flights from Mirinez. What's the name of the airport there?'

He stopped walking. He couldn't breathe now. He wasn't having another panic attack, but saying no just wasn't in his blood—not in his nature.

He tried to breathe out, to get rid of the choked feeling in his throat. His first thought had been that his father would never say no to a mission. He may not have been a doctor but as a commander, captain, then an admiral the US military had been in his blood.

He'd already stopped walking but now his feet were rooted to the ground. A cold breeze swept over him, chilling him more than it should.

But his father had said no. Of course he had.

When his mother had died his father had refused to be stationed anywhere without his son. It just hadn't really occurred to him before now what his father might *actually* have said no to.

Gibbs was still talking incessantly. 'Sullivan? Sullivan? Have we got a bad signal?'

Sullivan sucked in a deep breath. 'No.'

'No? You can hear me?'

'No, we don't have a bad signal. And, no, I'm sorry, I can't come. I'm not available.'

'You're not? But…' Gibbs sounded so stunned he just stopped in mid-sentence.

Sullivan still really, really wanted to say yes but he kept talking. 'Sorry, Gibbs. I've worked for almost three straight years. I need some time off. I need a break. I have a few things to sort out. I'll get back in touch with you when I'm ready to come back.' He closed his eyes as he kept talking. 'I will come back. I want to. I'll let you know when.'

He pulled the phone away from his ear and ended the call. He wasn't quite sure what else Gibbs would have said, but he knew he didn't need to hear it. He could claim a poor signal at a later date if need be.

What was important was he'd said no.

He stared at the phone for a second, then pressed the off switch. His hand gave the slightest shake. The urge to phone back was strong.

He looked over at the lights on in the clinic. He could see lots of people through the windows. Was the clinic usually this busy at night?

He strode across the road. He'd talk to Gabrielle soon. He'd tell her what he'd done, then figure out what came next.

For now, there were patients. And he was a doctor.

The waiting room was packed. She had two nurses working with her at the clinic. They were used to being here—she wasn't. The equipment in the community clinic was embarrassing, some so old it was falling apart. The prescription medicine cabinet only had the bare essentials. The computer system was antiquated. All things she would deal with.

It seemed that Sullivan had already had these thoughts. She'd found a list he'd started in the room he'd been working in.

It was long.

She'd worked in countries all over the world with less-than-perfect equipment—she just hadn't expected to find it here in Mirinez. A luxurious tax haven.

Her desk was covered with mounds of paper. 'What on earth are you doing, and who are all these patients?'

Sullivan was standing in the doorway, pointing out to the waiting room full of patients.

She ran her fingers through her hair. It had long escaped from the ponytail she'd tied on top of her head. She sighed and gave her eyes a rub. She was going to ask him for help. She had to. But was that fair?

'The case you thought was TB?'

He nodded as he walked across the room and stood at the other side of the desk.

She nodded her head. 'Oh, it's definitely TB. But when I took a history I realised I'd just opened a can of worms. I've found another five definite.' She rummaged through her paperwork. 'Twelve probable.' She held up her hand again. 'And about another twenty still to review.'

Her phone buzzed and she ignored it. He must have caught the expression on her face. 'Something else going on?'

She couldn't. She just couldn't tell him that. Probably because if he asked her a single question about her brother she was likely to dissolve into floods of tears. She had to be strong. She had to keep on top of things. How could she help Sullivan if she couldn't control her emotions?

She shook her head. 'Nothing I can't deal with.'

He picked up some of the paperwork. 'What do you need?'

Everything about this was wrong. That was the

question that she should be asking him right now, not the other way about. But what was worse was that she had to accept his help, even though she knew he needed help himself.

'Patient histories. Detailed patient histories. Chest X-rays read. Chests sounded. Treatment decisions—and maybe even a few admissions to hospital.'

She winced. 'My language skills haven't exactly helped. My Italian just isn't good enough. I don't speak Greek at all. As for Japanese? I just don't have a clue.' She was embarrassed to admit it. 'I've got one of the security guards out there, taking a history, because he knows a bit of Greek.'

Sullivan just gave a nod. But something was different. She could tell. When he'd been thrown into the breach in Narumba, into an area he'd been totally unfamiliar with, he'd been enthusiastic and motivated for the task. He hadn't worried about being a fish out of water. He'd just got on with things.

This time he just looked resigned to the fact he had to help. There wasn't the passion in his eyes. There wasn't the same cheeky glimmer.

She stood up and walked over, placing her hands on his chest.

'I'm sorry. I'm sorry I'm putting you in this position today. I know this isn't a good time.'

'What's that supposed to mean?' he snapped, then visibly winced at his own words and stepped back.

He looked wounded. 'Do you think I'm not capable of doing the job?'

She shook her head fiercely. 'Of course I don't. You're one of the best doctors I've ever worked with.' She couldn't hide the passion in her voice. She looked into his hurt pale green eyes. All she wanted to do was pull him closer, to wrap her arms around his neck and feel his heartbeat next to hers.

She lowered her voice. 'I want to keep working with you, Sullivan. I hope to keep working with you for a very long time.'

Her voice was trembling. It felt as if she was wearing her heart on her sleeve.

His gaze locked with hers. She stopped breathing. She just didn't know what would come next.

Her phone buzzed again and she could almost see the shutters coming down in his eyes. He picked up a pile of the paperwork. 'Let me deal with the Italian, Greek and Japanese patients. The histories and exams won't take long. I'll let you know if I have any queries or want to admit someone.'

The phone buzzing was incessant. Whatever it was, it wasn't going to go away.

He frowned. 'Is there something else?'

She shook her head automatically. 'No. Thanks so much for your help with this.'

He nodded and walked out the room.

Her heart squeezed inside her chest. Why did none of this feel right? She felt so torn. A country to serve. A man who deserved her support and love.

Why was it so hard to do both?

It was the oddest feeling in the world. He was talking to patients in multiple languages and taking patient histories. He listened to chests, reviewed X-rays, prescribed treatment regimes. He listened to their social problems around overcrowding and suitable housing and made multiple notes for Gabrielle.

He just had to look at her to know how much he wanted to be with her. But that only emphasised the numbness around his heart. It was almost as if it were encased with a wall of ice.

He wanted to think, he wanted to feel, he wanted to love. But now he'd realised how long he'd ignored his underlying grief, it had brought everything else to the surface. He had to move on.

He wanted to take the steps so he could plan for the future—plan for a future with Gabrielle.

He just couldn't find a way to put the words in his mouth. There were so many barriers. All his experience, all his medical training and he couldn't find the words. The weirdest thing of all was the fact that he knew that if he were the patient sitting in front of himself now—even though it wasn't his specialist area—he'd know exactly what to advise. It felt ironic that he actually had some insight into himself.

It was like everything had been brought to a head. Now he'd reached the point of realisation he had to act.

He signed his last prescription and checked the final set of notes.

He had to talk to Gabrielle. He had to tell her what he was going to do.

He loved her. He had to tell her that too.

But no. In order to feel free to love her, he had to deal with the things he'd pushed aside. The thought of going home made him feel sick. He'd avoided the place for so long and he'd built it up in his head so much that the thought of going back filled him with dread.

It was ridiculous—irrational—and he knew that.

How could he love Gabrielle when there was so much standing in his way?

And what if he couldn't shake off the aura that had surrounded him for the last few years? It didn't matter that he loved Gabrielle—was he truly worthy of her? Could he stand by her side and help her shoulder the burden of her role?

The truth was he wasn't sure. He had doubts. Not about Gabrielle, just about himself.

Was he really living up to the expectations that his father would have had of him? His insides coiled. He was letting down his father. He was letting down Gabrielle.

Right now, he couldn't give her any false hope, make any false promises.

The best thing he could do right now was leave.

He stood up and looked around the clinic. It was finally quiet.

He could hear Gabrielle's voice coming from the other room. She must still have a patient with her so he would have to wait until she was finished.

He tidied his paperwork and walked along the corridor. But Gabrielle's room was empty except for her. She was pacing back and forth, the phone pressed against her ear. 'What? How much? Have you spoken to the lawyers? What about the draft press statement that I prepared?' As he watched, a tear slid down her cheek. 'What do you mean, I'm not allowed to talk about it?'

She brushed the tear away angrily as she continued to pace. 'Is that what this has come to? I can be sued for how much?'

She stopped pacing. Her face was pale. He walked across the room towards her and put his hands on her shoulders, his expression asking the question for him.

She looked stricken but as soon as she realised he'd been listening she turned her back and walked away.

It was like a door slamming, being shut out completely. The person he wanted to reach out and actually talk to was obviously overwhelmed by something else entirely.

She didn't need any more pressure. She needed someone who could support her in the role she was struggling with. The last thing Gabrielle needed was a weight around her neck like Sullivan Darcy. At least that was how he felt at the moment.

What did he know about running a country?

He stepped back. The best thing he could do right now was give Gabrielle the space she needed to feel out her role.

He wanted to be the person by her side, but he didn't feel ready to offer her what she deserved. And whatever it was she was dealing with, it was obvious she didn't want to share it with him.

He gritted his teeth as she stood with her back to him, talking quietly.

He wasn't angry with her. He was angry with himself.

He'd never felt like this about someone before

and was almost overwhelmed by how much it took the breath from his lungs.

He wanted to be better for *her*.

She was still struggling with being Head of State. It could be that she'd decide this was a role she couldn't fulfil. He'd love her whatever her decision was. She wasn't Princess Gabrielle to him. She was just Gabrielle. And he'd take her in whatever form she came.

If she'd have him. But right now—this second? What could he offer her?

He took a deep breath.

It was time to take the steps to get better.

It was time to go.

The call took for ever. It seemed the palace legal advisors were very nervous about the outcome of the Prince Andreas situation.

She was furious. Frustrated. She didn't want to keep secrets. She hated being told that saying a single word about what had happened could lead to the palace being sued for millions.

She glanced over her shoulder. She felt so torn.

She wanted to deal with this. She wanted everything out in the open. She wanted Andreas held accountable for his actions. She wanted to be able to tell Sullivan what was going on.

Andreas should be punished. Those items didn't belong to him. Those jewels weren't his to take. And the money—the diverted funds—*definitely* weren't his to take. If she could climb on the plane to Bermuda right now and grab him with her own hands, she would.

But there was also a sinking feeling in her stomach. He could never come back now. The role of Head of State and Princess Gabrielle would always be hers.

It was a change of a whole mindset. A change of her life's ambitions.

But working alongside Sullivan towards the end of this week had made her realise that she could make the adjustments she needed. It might be tricky. It might be tough. But if she worked hard at the balance she should be able to work as a doctor as well as fulfil the role of Head of State.

But deep down she knew she wanted to do that with Sullivan by her side.

Working in the community clinic made her even more determined. She could see the holes in their current systems. She could work to change things and improve the healthcare for the general population. She didn't doubt Sullivan would want to help her with that. She would never ask him to give up his missions. Part of her ached that she wouldn't be able to do them any more.

But maybe he would be willing to combine time with her and time with Doctors Without

Borders. If they both wanted to, they could make this work.

The lawyer was still talking incessantly in her ear. She couldn't take another minute of this. She needed to talk to Sullivan. She cut him off. 'Check into our extradition treaties. I have no idea about them—but we must have some. Bermuda is a British overseas territory. If we don't have one, see if we can request Andreas's expulsion or lawful return. Find a way to make this work. If you need me to speak to the Governor, I will.'

She hung up the phone.

She needed to deal with this as quickly as possible. She wanted to spend time with Sullivan. She wanted to show him the same support that he'd shown her. It was obvious he'd been pushing things away for a long time. He needed someone by his side. Her heart and head told her that should be her.

She walked out of the office, her footsteps echoing through the clinic in an ominous way. 'Sullivan?'

The space seemed completely empty.

She glanced into the empty consulting room opposite her and walked through to the waiting room. One of the security staff was standing at the main door. 'Do you know where Sullivan is?'

He looked over his shoulder. 'He left ten minutes ago.'

Her stomach clenched. Something about this seemed wrong. It was the picture she had in her mind. The expression on his face. One part hurt, one part blankness.

'Did he say where he was going?'

The security guy shook his head. She walked back through to the office and picked up her bag. She'd arranged to admit three patients to one of the hospitals. Her medical instincts were over-whelming. She should go and speak to the staff about treatment plans, review their conditions.

One of the patients had been someone Sulli-van had assessed. It could be that he'd decided to go and follow up. But in her heart of hearts she knew he would have spoken to her if that had been his plan.

She climbed into the car outside the clinic. 'Take me back to the palace first. I'll go the hos-pital later.'

The driver nodded. She couldn't sit still. Her hands were shaking. She needed to speak to Sul-livan. She wanted to tell him that she loved him. She wanted to tell him she would be by his side the whole time.

By the time she reached the palace she could barely breathe. She ran inside and upstairs to where his apartments were. From the end of the corridor she could see the open door.

Her heart thudded in her chest as she reached

the bedroom. This time the cupboard doors were open. His suit and dress uniform were still hanging inside. The drawers in the dresser were empty, the bathroom bare.

Bile rose in the back of her throat.

Arun appeared at her side. 'Princess, is something wrong?'

She spun around. 'Where is he? Where has he gone?'

Arun winced. She could tell by one look that he knew everything.

He spoke carefully. 'He said he had something to deal with. Something he had to deal with on his own.' His voice softened. 'He's gone, Gabrielle. I'm sorry.'

She stepped back. It was the first time Arun had ever just called her by her name. He'd always used her title before.

She could see the sympathy on his face.

Tears welled up in her eyes. She couldn't do this without Sullivan. She didn't want to do this without him.

She clenched her fists. Andreas. This was all his fault. It wasn't enough that he'd tried to destroy their country. Now his behaviour could ruin her relationship with the man she loved.

She sucked in a deep breath.

No. No more.

Tears poured down her face. This wasn't really about Andreas.

This was about her.

She should have acted sooner. She should have told Sullivan how she felt about him. Asked him how he truly felt about her.

But now she knew.

The love she had in her heart for him wasn't echoed in his. Or, if it was, he still didn't want to be here with her.

He'd left with no explanation. He'd known she was busy. He hadn't even taken the time to talk to her.

But was that true?

He'd seen her on the phone. She'd been so overwhelmed she hadn't realised that those were the few seconds she'd really needed to break the call and talk to him.

Whether she'd meant to or not, she might have pushed him away.

She looked out of the window at the city below her. How on earth could she rule all of this? Her heart had hoped that Sullivan would be by her side. All the insecurities she'd had before were now bubbling to the surface.

It was time for her to take stock. To take charge.

To prioritise. She had to sort out her country. She had to function and serve as Head of State. It was time to fulfil the role that she'd inherited.

She watched the movement in the view below her. In a city full of people she'd never felt so alone.

She rubbed her hands up and down her arms as the tears continued to flow down her cheeks.

Alone.

The ache in her heart would never lessen.

She couldn't walk away from her country.

It seemed she had to walk away from her heart.

CHAPTER ELEVEN

TWENTY HOURS LATER he was beyond exhausted.

Stepping off the plane at almost four in the morning, Oregon time, he couldn't figure out if he should be awake or asleep.

The drive from the airport took just over an hour. The suburbs disappeared quickly, replaced by the rolling hills, greenery and trees he'd been so used to.

His stomach lurched as everything grew more familiar. Even though the temperature in the car hadn't changed, all the tiny hairs on the back of his neck stood on end.

As he ventured down the long drive he closed his eyes for the briefest of seconds. He just knew. He just knew as soon as he rounded the corner what he would see.

The traditional detached five-bed house sat on the edge of the scenic three-acre lake. The Cape Cod styled home with its wraparound porch and large single deck had a panoramic view of the lake, its large windows glinting in the orange sunrise. A three-stall horse barn with tack room and fenced pasture was behind the house, leading off to riding trails. It didn't matter the stalls had been empty for more than five years; if he breathed in right now, his senses would remember the smell. On the other side of the acreage was an orchard. Even from here he could see that his neighbour had kept good care of it after their handshake a few years ago.

As the car got closer, the details became clearer. The fishing dock at the front of house. The fire pit with custom pavers. The traditional dark wood door.

Perspiration started to trickle down his spine as he swung the car up in front of the house. He didn't want to get out. He didn't want to go inside.

His hands clenched the steering wheel and he just breathed. In. Out. In. Out.

The last time he'd actually gone to the diner just down the road and sat there for hours and hours. He'd eaten lunch and dinner, then nursed a cup of coffee that hadn't even been that good before he'd finally taken the road home under cover of darkness. He was tempted to do it all again today.

Gabrielle's face flashed in front of his face.

It was enough to make him open his eyes. He stared at one of the windows in the house. The pale yellow drapes moved a little. Was someone inside?

Before he knew it he was out of the car and

trying the front door. It didn't open. He rattled it. Then pulled the key from his pocket, turning it swiftly and stepping inside.

Silence. A waft of vanilla and peach. This wasn't the normal aroma of the house. Wood polish was what he remembered.

He looked around, holding his breath.

The sun was rising higher in the sky, sending a beam of light streaming through the window. Each window had a stained-glass inset at the top, and shards of shimmering green, purples and reds lit up the white walls around him.

Each footstep on the wooden floor echoed along the hallway. His head flicked from side to side, listening to the silence.

He strode through to the main room, eyes fixing on the curtains. There was still a tiny flicker of movement left in the yellow drapes. The room looked untouched. Comfortable cream recliners and sofas with wooden frames. Familiar paintings on the wall. If he closed his eyes right now he'd see his father sitting in his favourite chair.

His skin on his right arm prickled. He felt air. A breeze, carrying in the smell of peaches and vanilla from the orchard outside.

He turned and strode through to the kitchen. There. A small hopper window was open at the back of the house near the orchard, letting fresh air into the room. His finger ran along the counter top and he frowned as he looked at it.

Clean. No dust.

What the…?

Something washed over him. A realisation. When he'd shaken hands with his neighbour about the orchard he'd handed over an emergency key, just in case of fire or flood. Matt's wife, Alice, obviously occasionally looked over the place. They were a kind-hearted young couple who'd moved here with their kids to build a new life. His dad had liked them immediately. He would have to say thank you.

He stared about him. The maple staircase was almost beckoning. Calling him upstairs. His muscles tensed. So many memories were all around.

He moved to the foot of the stairs and rested his palm on the hand rail. His body jerked. An involuntary action. As if someone had just stuck their hand through his chest and grabbed hold of his heart with an icy grasp.

I can do this. I can do this. I can do this.

He started whispering the mantra out loud that was echoing around his head.

He'd done this before. He'd been up the stairs in the house after his father had died. He'd spent the night here before. Had he slept? Not a bit.

None of these were first times.

But he'd been so shuttered. It was almost like

walking around in a plastic bubble, storing all the emotions inside so tightly it was almost as if they weren't there.

Today his emotions were front and centre. There was no barrier. No camouflage.

His hand trembled on the rail. His feet started moving slowly and steadily up the stairs. There was nothing to fear up here. There was no bogeyman. No axe murderer.

There were just a million memories of a man he'd loved and adored.

A father who'd centred his life around his son. Who'd adjusted his career. Who'd told him a thousand stories about his mother to try and keep her memory alive. There had never been a step-mom. His dad had always said his heart belonged to one woman.

And Sullivan understood that now.

He'd met Gabrielle. The picture in his head was of her dancing in the tent in her cut-off shorts and pink T-shirt, shimmying to the music. Even now it brought a smile to his lips. He wanted to get to the point where he could tell Gabrielle what she was to him. That she was the sun, moon and stars—never mind a princess. He had no idea if she would find him worthy. He could only live in hope.

His feet were still moving, automatically taking him to the door of his father's room. It was wide open, inviting him in.

There was no aroma of peaches and vanilla up here.

He moved slowly across the room. His hand shook as he reached for the handle on the wardrobe. He jerked it open and within seconds the smell hit him full in the face.

He staggered, not quite ready to deal with the overwhelming rush of feeling that flooded through his system.

There were all the clothes. Hanging there, waiting. Waiting for his father to reach out and pick something out to put on. The button-down shirts. The pants. The jackets.

And the uniforms.

He reached out and touched the blue sleeve. The feel of the fabric shot a pulse of memories straight to his brain. He could see his father's smile and laughing eyes as he'd proudly worn the dress uniform. If he went downstairs right now he'd find a hundred pictures of the two of them in uniform together. His father had once made it out to Helmand Province. His all-time favourite picture of them both was one that a friend had snapped with a phone. It was of the two of them sitting on a block of concrete surrounded by the dirt of Afghanistan, hats at their feet and laughing as if a famous comedian was putting on a private show for them both.

One snap immortalised their whole relationship for Sullivan. Fun, love and mutual respect.

He staggered backwards and landed on the bed.

And then he sobbed.

CHAPTER TWELVE

HER HEART WAS wound so tightly in her chest it felt as if it could explode.

Three weeks. Three weeks of hearing nothing from Sullivan. She was pretty sure that he'd turned his phone off.

Arun had tracked his flights. She didn't know how and she wasn't going to ask any questions but Sullivan had gone to the place he should have— home.

Sleep had been a complete stranger these last three weeks. The first night she could smell his aftershave on the neighbouring pillow. She'd swapped it immediately with her own then had spent the rest of night hanging onto it for dear life.

She was determined. She had a duty, one that she would fulfil.

But she had another duty, one for herself and the man she loved.

Her rigid stance and feisty personality had meant that for the last few weeks her palace staff had seen a whole new side to Princess Gabrielle.

The advisors and lawyers were now firmly in their places.

But Gabrielle had discovered skills she hadn't even known she possessed. She'd been determined Andreas was going to be held to account for his actions and, thankfully, the government in Bermuda agreed.

She strode through to the room that had been specially set up in the palace. Her dark curls were pinned back into a bun and she'd asked for her make-up to be heavier than normal. She wanted her appearance to reflect exactly how she was feeling. This situation was serious.

She nodded at Franz. 'Everything ready?'

A look of panic crossed his face. He turned to the director. 'Well, we have to practise lighting and sound checks and set-up and—'

Gabrielle held up her hand. She narrowed her eyes and looked at the director. 'I expect all of these things to have been carried out. I'm ready. Are you?'

The room was silent. She walked around to the desk set up in front of the camera and sat down, taking a few seconds to adjust the seat and microphone.

She looked straight into the camera. 'There's no rehearsal. I don't need one. Let's begin.'

There was a flurry of activity. People took their places instantly. She wasn't trying to be scary. She was just trying to be direct. Her patience was spent.

After a couple of minutes the director gave her a nod. 'Princess Gabrielle, if you're ready, we're ready. I'll count you down.'

She nodded. The director gave a wave and spoke loudly. 'Three, two, one and go.'

Gabrielle took a deep breath. Her heart was thumping wildly but everything in her head was crystal clear.

'Good evening, citizens of Mirinez. As you know, I'm Princess Gabrielle, your new Head of State. You are all aware that this role is new to me. I've spent the last three years working as a physician specialising in TB medicine for Doctors Without Borders in various places across the world. I never thought the role of Head of State in Mirinez would be one I would have to fulfil. However, with the abdication of Prince Andreas, I have been called into service—this is a role I take seriously and am fully committed to.

'On my arrival back in Mirinez I discovered that a number of duties normally carried out by the Head of State had been neglected. I want to assure you all that since I've arrived, all outstanding matters of state have been dealt with. Unfortunately, I also discovered that some funds had been misappropriated and some national treasures belonging to Mirinez had disappeared. A full inventory has been taken. I've also requested a full and independent investigation of all accounting irregularities. After taking legal advice, a warrant for the arrest and a request for the extradition of Andreas Cartier was made to the government in Bermuda.'

Gabrielle stopped to take a deep breath.

'The warrant was served a few hours ago, the request for extradition granted and arrangements are now being made for the return of Andreas Cartier to Mirinez. A number of items missing from state have also been recovered.'

She kept her back ramrod-straight and didn't let any emotion show on her face.

'Andreas Cartier will be held to account for his actions, just as any citizen of Mirinez would be.'

She licked her lips.

'When I returned to Mirinez many of you will know that I had a friend—a companion—with me. Sullivan Darcy, a respected surgeon and colleague at Doctors Without Borders, helped with this transition in my life. He also assisted at the mining accident, operating on a number of patients. It is my intention to continue working as a doctor, as well as functioning as Head of State. I think that the two duties complement each other and will allow me to keep in touch with our citizens in the most fundamental way—by serving them at one of our community clinics.'

She felt her muscles relax a little, her expression soften.

'I will be gone for the next few days. But I can assure you all matters of state are in hand. What I need to do now is personal. I need to deal with some affairs of the heart.'

She couldn't help but give a small hopeful smile as she ignored all the chins bouncing off the floor in the room around her.

'When I return I will make arrangements for my dual role. And perhaps I will have some other news for the citizens of Mirinez. I ask you all to have patience with me in my time of transition and know that I am committed to doing the best job possible.'

Gabrielle stood up and walked out. Questions raged all around her. But Arun was waiting at the door.

She had one thing on her mind. She'd more or less just worn her heart on her sleeve for the entire world to see.

But she'd meant every word.

It was time to put her heart first. It was time to reach out to the person she loved and be there for him. She'd no idea what he'd say when she got there. She'd no idea what she'd find. But it was time to find out.

Three long weeks. That's how long it had taken to get to this point.

And it had been the longest three weeks of her life.

All the arrangements were in place.

She met Arun's gaze and he gave the briefest nod of his head, and spirited her away.

CHAPTER THIRTEEN

HE'D STARTED TO appreciate the silence. He'd spent so much of his life surrounded by noise and confusion that the silence of the lake was washing over him like a soothing balm. He'd spent the first night sleeping in his father's bed. What amazed him most was that he'd managed a few hours of actual sleep. But he'd woken with the biggest crick in his back in the world. It was clear the mattress needed replacing.

Yesterday he'd managed to take a few things from the wardrobe and chest of drawers and pack them up for goodwill. That had been hard. Every cardigan, every shirt brought back a flash of memory. The uniforms still hung in place. He'd get to them. He would. Just not yet. He wasn't quite ready.

Last week he'd walked around the empty stables. He'd never had a horse. Horses had been his mother's love. But it seemed such a shame that perfectly good stables and paddock were empty.

He'd spent the afternoon nursing a beer, sitting near the orchard and letting the smells of the fruit drift around him.

Today he'd walked over to meet his neighbours. Their children had grown rapidly and it was clear they'd added another as a pram was parked at their front door. He'd welcomed the family's noise around him as they'd chatted about future plans for the orchard.

Tonight he was watching the lake. There were a few boats out there, a few people fishing along the shore. He'd never been much of a fisherman and preferred to just sit with his legs swinging from the dock, contemplating whether he should take a look at the fire pit.

He hadn't turned his phone back on. There was always the chance that Gibbs would call again. He was sure Gabrielle would have called and that made his chest hurt. He wouldn't hide from Gabrielle—not like he'd hidden from this. But a few weeks in Oregon wouldn't fix him. It was just the first steps of a process. The thoughts of a counsellor were now chasing around his head. Some people would classify not dealing with grief as a kind of depression.

Sullivan had thought about it and didn't want to go down a medication route—not even for his lack of sleep. He wanted to deal with this in his own way.

He turned around the looked at the house. The lights were on inside, giving it a warm glow in the dimming evening light. He liked it that way.

Any minute now his dad would appear, fold his arms, lean on the doorjamb and ask who was making dinner.

His mouth dried instantly. He took another swig of beer from the chilled bottle in his hand. The memories would always be there. The last thing he wanted to do was chase them away. What he had to learn to do now was let them warm him, instead of leaving him feeling cold.

The emptiness that had been there the last three years didn't seem quite so hollow now.

Gabrielle.

His father would have adored her. He wouldn't quite have believed that Sullivan had not only met a beautiful, courageous fellow doctor but that she'd actually been a secret royal. His father would have spent a lifetime teasing him about that.

Would his father have thought him worthy of Gabrielle? Now he'd started the healing process he could finally be more positive. His father would have encouraged him to find love. Wherever it was.

He looked down at the water rippling around his feet. There was something so reassuring about knowing that the two people he'd loved most in this world would probably have loved each other too. He could picture them all, sitting around the neglected fire pit while his father told her stories of long-ago missions and his clashes with a few well-known characters.

This morning he'd found a black velvet box tucked inside one of his father's shoes. Another of his quirks. It held a ring—a square emerald with a diamond on either side. There had been a tiny folded-up piece of paper inside with his father's writing.

Sullivan—for whoever the next Mrs Darcy might be.

That was all it had said. Nothing more. They'd never had a conversation about his mother's engagement ring. He'd always assumed his mother had been wearing it when she'd been buried. His father had never mentioned it. Never asked if he was planning on having a wife, or a family. Never put any pressure on his son. But the thoughts had obviously been there.

He'd left the ring in the shoe for now. There was only one finger he'd ever want to put it on. And a princess like Gabrielle would probably have a huge amount of jewellery that would be worth so much more.

But when the time was right, he would use the ring to ask the question.

He just wasn't sure when that would be.

* * *

Gabrielle was beyond tired. The voice on the satnav was grating. Honestly, if she could meet the person who had that voice, chances were she'd close her hands around their throat. How could you take the next road on the right when it didn't exist?

She'd finally turned it off and just gone with her instincts. Oregon was so much bigger than she'd anticipated, the scenery unexpected.

Rolling green hills, deep valleys, lakes and trees—everywhere. It took some time to get her bearings. The road was lined with trees. There was a calmness about this country, something that just seemed so right.

After about a mile she could see the house ahead emerging through the trees. It was large but inviting, set on the shore of a lake. Her heart leapt in her chest. Even from here she could see the orange lights and the figure sitting on the dock, nursing a beer.

Everything she had ever wanted.

That was her first thought. That was her only thought.

But did he want her?

His head tilted as he heard the noise of the car. He didn't get up, just stayed where he was, smiling.

She pulled the car up outside the house and

opened the door. The warm Oregon air surrounded her, welcoming her, while her stomach did huge somersaults.

In her head she would have liked a chance to change and reapply her lipstick. But the world had a different idea. So she pulled her wrinkled yellow patterned dress from her thighs and let the air drift around her.

She wasn't as terrified as she'd been before. Just being near Sullivan had that effect on her. Even without a word being spoken.

She strolled over to where he sat.

'Hi.' She might not be terrified, but she was still nervous.

'Hi.' There was warmth in his eyes. Calmness.

'Got another one of those?'

'I might have.' He leaned down into the lake at his feet and pulled up another bottle of beer from the water, knocking the cap off on the side of the dock.

She smiled as she kicked off her sandals and sat down next to him, letting out a gasp as her toes touched the water.

He laughed. 'I keep it a special temperature—all for cooling beer.'

'I think you do.' Now she was here, all the great speeches and declarations she'd conjured up in her head seemed to drift up into the purple clouds above them, floating off and laughing at her.

'How are you?' It seemed the best way to start.

He went to answer immediately then stopped. She watched him while her heart played around in her chest. 'I haven't found out yet,' he answered.

She nodded and took a swig from the chilled beer bottle. It was a welcome relief after the long hours of travel. 'Neither have I,' she agreed.

He glanced at her curiously. 'What have you been up to?'

There was no animosity. Just curiosity. He'd obviously wondered what had been happening since he'd left.

She stared out across the lake, reflecting a myriad of colours from the setting sun above. 'You haven't seen the news?'

He gave a half-laugh. 'Haven't you heard? I've put myself in solitude for a while.' He held up his hands. 'Consider this a media-free zone.'

She looked from side to side. 'Seems you picked a prime location.'

He nodded appreciatively. 'I certainly did.'

They sat in silence for a few seconds. It was beautiful here. She hadn't really taken the time to picture this place in her head at all. There hadn't been time. But now she was here? It was like their own little private haven. Secluded from all but a select few.

She pressed her lips together and gave a kind of wry smile.

'I caused a bit of a stir.'

He raised his eyebrows. 'What now?'

His rich voice sent pulses through her body. She locked gazes with him. 'I might have declared that I love you on TV.'

His eyebrows rose. 'You what?'

She stared at her beer for a second. Talking into the camera had seemed easier than this. Impersonal. It wasn't impersonal now.

'I decided some things were worth fighting for.'

His eyes widened and he stared. 'I'm not sure I'm worth fighting for yet.'

She could see confusion in his eyes. Self-doubt.

She held up her hands. 'You're here. You've taken the first step. Let me take the walk with you.'

She could see him swallow. He took a long time to answer. 'I want to tell you something, Gabrielle. I don't have a single doubt in my head or heart how I feel about you. I love you, I know that.' He pressed his hand against his chest. 'But I've shut out some things for so long that I feel unreliable. I've spent so long *not* feeling that it seems as though I have to deal with myself first before I try to move forward.'

She nodded. He'd said the words. He'd said the

words she wanted to hear. She should be skipping.
She should be happy. And she knew he was sincere. But she also understood.

'Why now?'

He nodded and gave her a rueful kind of smile.
'I guess I wasn't ready before. I think I probably
didn't have someone to fight for. I was too busy
pushing things away, wallowing, I suppose. I hate
myself for that.'

She could see the self-contempt on his face.
But he wanted to fight for her. That made her
want to sing and shout to the world. 'It's called
grief, Sullivan. Don't hate yourself. I have something to fight for too. You. Us. This is where I
want to be. I love you too.' She held up her hands
and smiled. 'I've told the world.'

She slid her fingers through his, intertwining
their hands above his heart.

He met her gaze with his pale green eyes. 'I'm
here. But I won't feel better overnight. I have
some work to do.'

She nodded. 'And I'll be by your side.' She
smiled and tilted her head to the side. 'You saved
me, Sullivan. You saved me when I needed it
most. You saved me when I was ready to walk
away and forget everything. You helped me see
that I could do both jobs.' She closed her eyes for
a second. 'Hopefully, well.' Then she shook her
head. 'But I don't want to do either of them with-

out you. The last three weeks have clarified that
for me. I care, Sullivan. I want you to feel well.
I want you to get the help you need to say good-
bye to your dad.' She reached over and touched
his cheek. 'And something you don't know about
me is that I'm patient. I can wait.'

He raised his eyebrows. 'Patient? You? Since
when?'

She was glad he could still joke with her. She
kept her hand where it was. 'I won't pretend this
will be easy. You may see a lot of tears. The news
I couldn't tell you before was the other part of
my speech. Andreas stole from Mirinez. Money,
artefacts, who knows what else. After some ne-
gotiations he'll be extradited from Bermuda. I'll
have to watch my brother be tried in court and
sent to prison. I won't pretend with you that in
private I won't be breaking my heart and be sob-
bing about it.'

'Why didn't you tell me?'

She shook her head slowly. 'I was trying to
take it all in. I didn't want to believe it at first.
The palace advisors kept telling me not to discuss
anything. I didn't know what to do.'

'And now you do?'

She smiled. 'I'm starting to find my feet. I'm
hoping someone else will be able to give me a
bit of balance.'

He turned his head to watch the rippling lake. 'Do you really think we can make this work?'

She nudged him with her shoulder. 'I think this will be messy. I missed you. You've only been gone three weeks. What happens when you're away on a mission?'

It was reality. She knew that once Sullivan felt better he would want to return to work. She'd never stop him. But it would be hard. It was best just to lay it all on the line.

He nodded slowly. 'That's part of the reason my phone's still off. I'm avoiding Gibbs.' He turned towards her. 'There's work to be done in Mirinez at the community clinics. People without insurance will still need surgery. I'd like to think that I can work between Doctors without Borders and the community clinics.'

'You'd do that?' Her heart swelled up in her chest. If Sullivan worked between both, it meant they'd actually spend some time together. Missing him would be hard but knowing he'd be back to work with her would make it so much easier.

His expression was so sincere. 'Of course. If you want me to.' He gave her a smile. 'I can't imagine a day without you, Gabrielle. I just had to know that I had something to offer you.'

She moved, putting both hands around his neck. 'You saved me, Dr Darcy. How about you let me save you right back?'

He smiled as he slid her arms around her waist. 'That sounds like some kind of deal. But how do we seal it?'

She slid her hands through his hair, 'Oh, there's only one way to seal this.' And she tilted her chin up and put her lips to his as the setting sun sent the last of its orange and red rays spilling across the lake.

EPILOGUE

Two years later

'READY?' ADMIRAL SANDS looked even more nervous than she was as he tilted his arm towards her.

She straightened her veil and took a deep breath. 'Absolutely.'

He'd been the perfect choice to walk her down the aisle. With her own father dead and her brother in prison, her options had been somewhat limited. But Joe Sands had been a great support during Sullivan's recovery and he'd become one of their greatest friends. It was the first time in the history of Mirinez that someone had given the bride away and also played the role of best man.

He leaned forward and whispered, 'You look absolutely beautiful, Your Highness. I'm so proud of you both.'

She stood on tiptoe and kissed him on the cheek. 'Thank you, Joe.'

He signalled to the staff at the door of the royal cathedral. The trumpets sounded as the doors opened and they started to walk down the red carpet.

The cathedral was packed. So much for the quiet wedding they'd both wanted.

One of Mirinez's tiaras glittered on her head, as well as the emerald and diamond engagement ring glittering on her finger. She'd been so touched when Sullivan had proposed with his mother's ring. It had made their closeness even more complete.

Her gown was traditional, covered in lace made by traditional lace-makers in Mirinez, with a long sweeping train. Thank goodness they'd chosen the cooler spring for their wedding instead of summer.

Sullivan was waiting at the top of the aisle. Breaking with tradition, he turned to watch her coming towards him. In his dress uniform, with his tan from his recent mission, she'd never seen him looking so handsome. His face had filled out a little in the last couple of years and she could see the gleam in his pale green eyes even from where she was. That man was so sexy.

She couldn't wait to be his wife.

It was almost like he'd read her mind.

He started walking towards her, ignoring the sharp intake of breath from the wedding guests in the cathedral.

Joe Sands started laughing. 'Never could tell that boy what to do.'

He met them halfway up the aisle. 'What are you doing?' she whispered.

'This,' he said with a grin that spread from ear to ear, putting his hands around her waist, tilting her backwards and putting his lips to hers.

It was a kiss that promised everything. And spoke of the journey they'd taken. Sullivan starting back at work. His ever-steady presence during her brother's trial and conviction. The new radical decisions she'd taken about developing Mirinez's own health service for its citizens. And the joy she'd felt waking up next to the man she loved. She pulled her lips back for a second. 'We're causing a scandal.' She couldn't help but smile.

'Just wait until they find out about the twins,' he whispered in her ear as he eased her back up and took her other arm.

She winked at him as she smiled at the men on either side of her.

'Gentlemen, shall we? I think we have a wedding to attend.'

All three of them laughed. And that was the picture that made the headlines the next day across the world.

* * * * *

*If you enjoyed this story, check out these
other great reads from Scarlet Wilson*

**A ROYAL BABY FOR CHRISTMAS
ONE KISS IN TOKYO
THE DOCTOR'S BABY SECRET
A TOUCH OF CHRISTMAS MAGIC**

All available now!